W hat critics are saying about Michael Phillip Cash's work:

Brood X: A Firsthand Account of the Great Cicada Invasion
Reviews

"Part satiric take on contemporary yuppie expectations... part anatomization of contemporary marriage...part creature-feature with all of the traditional elements of the great 50s films...part homage to the fairly recent genre of found-footage horror films--Brood X is a quick, fun read."
- Michael R. Collings - hellnotes.com

"...a Twilight Zone-like horror story of biblical proportions."
- Mark McLaughlin - ForeWord Reviews

"...horror at its best...up close and personal, and inflicted with ways that address humanity's inherent fear of and disgust for bugs." - Mark McLaughlin - ForeWord Reviews

"breathing new life into a genre that has been occupied too long by the usual suspects: sickness, the undead and global warming." - **Kirkus Reviews**

Brood X- 1st Place Winner Mystery/ Thriller Rebecca's Reads Readers Choice Awards

Brood X-Winner Readers Views Literary Awards 2013

Stillwell: A Haunting on Long Island Reviews

"Cash easily draws readers into the story by creating three-dimensional characters who are easy to care about." **- ForeWord Reviews**

"With strong characters and a twist unexpected in a thriller, this book is an enjoyable beach read." **- ForeWord Reviews**

"A horror tale with well-developed characters..." **- Kirkus Review**

"I do not see what would stop Michael Phillip Cash's horror masterpiece from becoming a bestseller." - **pjtheemt. blogspot.com**

ForeWord Reviews
2013 Book of the Year Award
Finalist
Horror

Stillwell won honorable mention for General Fiction in the Rebecca's Reads Choice Awards 2013!

The Hanging Tree- A Novella
Reviews

"This fast paced novella, easily read in one sitting, spins a tale of woe dating back to 1649, when a woman wrongly accused of witchcraft curses the reverend who sentenced her to death. As the years roll by, a number of his descendants fall victim to the curse and find themselves inhabitants of the hanging tree. The story's greatest strengths are its pacing and structure: Each short chapter develops an individual victim's back story piece by piece, leaving readers in constant, eager anticipation..." - **Kirkus Reviews**

"A short but mesmerizing tale, this spine tingling test of the human spirit quite literally takes on the ghosts of our ancestors in an attempt to neutralize their mistakes." - **ForeWord Review**

ForeWord Reviews
2013 Book of the Year Award
Finalist
Horror

Schism The Battle for Darracia
<u>*Reviews*</u>

"*The writing is smooth and builds nicely; creating an engaging tale with a big bang ending that leaves you thankful it is the beginning of a series. Definitely recommended for fans of dystopian novels in want of a fast page-turning read.*" - **The Children's Book Review**

"*This coming-of-age fantasy novel with a subtle sci-fi backdrop follows a half-breed prince who's forced to embrace his unique identity when his intolerant uncle - vehemently set against a looming peace accord between antagonistic races - attempts to usurp his father's throne...the briskly paced storyline features a cast of well-developed characters...Well-written...a solid foundation for what could be an excellent series.*" - **Kirkus Review**

"*...a fast-paced novel that will appeal to lovers of science fiction and fantasy. Set on an alien planet, this is a story about social equality and the struggles faced by those seeking great change....The author has crafted a complex society with a well-defined class system facing a political struggle for social equality. This is the first installment of a planned* *series, and Cash does a fine job laying the groundwork for future books. Schism is a quick, pleasurable read that is sure to entertain."* - **ForeWord Reviews**

**ForeWord Reviews
2013 Book of the Year Award
Finalist
Science Fiction**

Winner 2nd Place for Science Fiction from Rebecca's Reads Choice Awards 2013!

Collision: The Battle for Darracia (Book II) Reviews

"Collision is an entertaining novel that continues the story of V'sair and his struggle to unite the races on the planet of Darracia. Packed with action, political intrigue, love, and betrayal, Michael Phillip Cash's book will appeal to a wide audience, particularly fans of science fiction." - **ForeWord Review**

"Collision is a complex, spanning multiple worlds with their own economies, mythologies, and customs. The descriptions are delightful and vivid, painting clear pictures that help to define both the characters and their worlds." - **ForeWord Review**

Dedication

*To my grandparents
I can't see you but I know you are always
there.*

All along the untrodden paths of the future, I can see the footprints of an unseen hand.

- **Boyle Roche**

Prologue

"**I** hate this place," Brad grumbled, as he shoved another piece of crap into the superthick black garbage bag. The basement smelled like shit, and here he was, alone on his birthday and shoveling hundred-year-old junk from a dank cellar. This had to be the worst flip they'd ever attempted. He gave the creaky stairs a gimlet-eyed glance and for a nanosecond hated Julie. Really hated her and her cockamamie ideas. *Where did that idea of hate come from?* he wondered. He loved his wife, didn't he?

"It has so much charm," she'd cooed every time they discussed the place. And then, last night, she'd sprung it on him. "Let's keep it."

"Over my dead body," he told the decaying piles of newspaper. Once they finished this job and paid their bills, he had some thinking to do. She picked the homes, went back to her tidy little job in the city, and left him to muck around in the garbage. He couldn't see himself doing this for the next twenty years, not anymore. Not after this dump. It wasn't that he was afraid of work, or even plain old elbow grease. There was something about this project that turned him off. From the moment he entered the house, his skin crawled, and he found himself unaccountably angered by Julie and her insistence that they buy this place. It was as though his opinions didn't count, and she made him feel like a hired hand instead of her partner.

He poked his shovel into the corner; then, satisfied nothing lived there, dug deep into someone's discarded life to make room for the next person to live in the house.

"Want to have some fun?" It was the faintest whisper, very feminine, spectral, and light; it danced on the breeze made by the cheap fan he had put down there to circulate the fetid air. Brad didn't hear it—maybe a light tickle around the shell of his ear—but someone else did.

"He is a handsome one," the female voice said, continuing the conversation.

"Don't start that again. I don't want them here. They are an intrusion. Look what he's doing," a male voice replied, and took on a menacing growl.

Brad stopped, a sudden chill making the hairs on his arm stand up. He wiped the sweat from his brow and shuddered. His gray eyes narrowed as he scanned the room. Satisfied, he shrugged and removed a rubber band from the pocket of his jeans to make a ponytail. He had long light-brown hair that tended to bleach itself blond in the sun. It was just long enough to graze his shoulders. It drove his father-in-law crazy, and he liked that, he thought with a smile.

"I can wipe that smile off his face in a second," the frustrated male said.

"Stop!" An elegant hand stayed him. "Really, stop, Gerald. I like him." It was obvious Tessa liked him. She couldn't take her eyes off his body. She swirled around him. Gerald hated her sighs of delight. Gerald called her name but was ignored, his fury growing when Tessa swiped her hand down the intruder's backside. The man straightened, looked stupidly around, and then went back to his incessant shoveling.

"Well, I don't! You always like them, especially when they are male." With that, a small whirlpool of air eddied into a mini tornado, stirring up the neat piles Brad had created.

Brad jumped back as papers flew around the room. "What the…?" He stared, his mouth open, blinking his eyes. The papers floated gracefully to land in a new mess at his booted feet. He turned to look at the fan, docilely rotating right, then left, and then back to the new mess. "What was that?" he asked no one in particular, eyeing the stairs with a venomous glare once again. He felt itchy under his own skin, his anger bubbling through his veins. Never short-tempered, the feeling irritated him, making him cranky and uncomfortable. Rolling his shoulders, he picked up a broom, leaning against a wall, to push the mess forcefully into a pile. Yep, he and Julie were going to have a little talk, and that talk was going to be tonight.

CHAPTER ONE

J ulie hung up the phone with a satisfied snap. This would make her boss happy. She had collected on an old debt, one the firm had given up on. That was her charm, her boss often told her: she was as tenacious as a terrier. She wasn't quite sure if that was a compliment or not, being compared to a dog, but she'd take it. The job was, well, OK. She thought that her boss believed he paid her enough, but that was open for discussion as far as she was concerned. She had been there since graduating college. After majoring in psychology, there wasn't much she could find out in the workplace, so she stayed. She had started as the receptionist, then moved to DocStar, filing boring information all day, and now she had settled into the collection department, doubling as an assistant to the boss. Oh, he had a secretary—she had been with him for over twenty years—but they gave the grunt work to Julie. She wondered who was crankier: Mr. Wilson, her boss, or Joanne, his right hand. The older woman had iron-gray hair to match an iron spine, and every so often, Julie wanted to ask if she removed the rod up her ass when she went to sleep at night.

She owed Mr. Wilson a lot. When she had entered the flipping business, he arranged for her first loans. He liked her ambition, he told her. He respected the fact that she was willing to work at her small business on the weekends. Mr. Wilson supported free enterprise, as long as it didn't interfere with Julie's day job. While he hadn't given her a raise in eight years, doing this side business had enabled her to make up the difference. It had started with a condo in Rego Park. It was a foreclosure Mr. Wilson had told her about. She bought it, resurfaced the kitchen, cleaned up the cat shit, and sold it, making herself a clean $15,000. Flipping was easy. Buy a house that needed some lipstick, clean it up, and sell it, making a small amount of money for the next one. The collapsed economy was a perfect excuse for her boss to freeze her salary, but he had made up for it when he found a second property for her and set Julie up with a decent contractor. When she met Brad, they eighty-sixed the hired help and did the work themselves.

Getting ahead was tough, but doing this side venture made her a little independent. Each flip was still a struggle. One mistake, such as wood rot she wasn't prepared for or hidden problems missed on the primary inspections, could throw her whole bottom line out the window. Julie didn't have a big war chest, as her father called it. In other words, she had very little in reserve. Each job represented a hard-earned profit that enabled her to invest in another property right after. Still, she had trouble landing funds. The whole banking industry was a mess after the mortgage meltdown. They were so careful with whom they did business, making borrowing money very difficult. She had no assets, nothing to secure for a big credit line to purchase the houses. Mr. Wilson not only cosigned for her, but he also pushed the bank to give her more credit. He was the bank's biggest customer and had enough clout there to bully them around. And one thing was certain: Mr. Wilson was a bully. Brad didn't like her boss. Lately, it seemed that Brad didn't like anything connected to her.

She frowned, new worry lines creasing the smooth skin of her brow. She was pretty, not beautiful. Cute, perky, with long brown hair kissed by the sun, a swinging body toned with hours of yoga, and merry green eyes. The people who liked her said she was a go-getter; the ones who didn't said she had a type A personality. Brad told her he liked her drive, found her inspiring, and enjoyed their chemistry. His laconic attitude tempered her impulsiveness. Their fundamental differences enhanced each other, creating a perfect balance. Holding up her wedding photo, she stared wistfully at the tanned couple. They looked perfect together. He was wearing a slick white dinner jacket with black tuxedo pants. She wore a Calvin Klein slip of a dress. They were both barefoot and ankle-deep in the sands of a Dominican Republic beach. The wind had snatched her veil. Brad's arms were protectively around her when the photographer had snapped a classic black-and-white shot of them on the beach. She loved that picture; it summed up the simplicity of her relationship with Brad. It was black and white, no bullshit, founded in love, rooted in respect, and a whole lot of fun. In other words, it was bliss. They looked like a couple from a high-end perfume advertisement, everybody always said.

Theirs had been a wonderful storybook courtship. Boy meets girl, instant attraction, destination: wedding. They had met at one of those Match.com mixers and hit it off immediately. She couldn't believe he wasn't taken. He had shoulders that filled a room, as well as a personality to match. He had just left the army after two tours in Afghanistan, and compared to the guys she normally dated, he was the real deal. Kind, polite, and ever so gallant, it didn't take her long to let every rule fall by the wayside and allow herself to commit early. If only he could find something he liked to do. After his discharge, he drove a limo on the weekends while he attended a community college. She knew he disliked it, and after they dated a bit, she had talked him into flipping houses with her. They had split the cost of three houses, small tract homes in Levittown, nothing so big that they could get hurt.

Julie did all the legwork. She had loads of time to do that in the office and evenings. The Internet was her best friend, making it easy for her to do research on what they needed. Brad was a worker. There was nothing he wouldn't try to do. He wasn't in love with the work— sometimes she felt guilty knowing he was hip-deep in hoarder hell, shoveling accumulated crap into a rented Dumpster. He fumigated homes, was the resident rat catcher, cleaned the toxic bathrooms. Brad never complained, but she could see the resigned look on his face when he began to tackle a new purchase. He had this vast store of common sense on how to fix things like broken outlets or stubborn plumbing. He could take a few tools and tinker with problems, finding ways for them to save money by rescuing projects others would just discard. He was the most patient person she had ever met. It seemed that was when he was happiest, taking a lost cause and using his skill to restore and reuse. His Yankee ingenuity had doubled their profits. Where Julie saw garbage or a jumble of wires, Brad saw a challenge to bring it back to life. Brad wasted nothing. He cleaned the houses, carted out the junk, and sold what they could salvage, then hung drywall, put in bathrooms with an army buddy, and one time even did a wooden planked floor. He was meticulous, taking his time while she constantly reminded him they were under the gun to do the job quickly.

Did they clash? Not really. He would give a lazy grin when Julie went off on a rant. It didn't take long for her to lose steam, distracted by his charming smile and smoky eyes. Brad knew exactly how to defuse her energy, making her forget timetables and deadlines; she learned that things got done when they got done and that bottom lines could be adjusted. They had turned a tidy profit, and he had proposed in the last house. Julie's eyes filled while she remembered how he had prepared a path of rose petals and illuminated the empty living room with dozens of glowing tea lights. He had set up a small bridge table and prepared a feast of lobsters from his native Maine, along with all the other goodies that come with a clambake. The ring was small but oh so beautiful—an antique Edwardian with tiny sapphires surrounding a small rose-cut diamond. She loved that ring, and when he went down on one knee, she launched herself onto his deep chest, vowing never to leave. Julie shivered in her seat, her face flushed, her lips tingling, thinking of Brad and the wicked way he told her how much he loved her. Her brows drew together as her lips pursed. It had been a long time since he'd done those things to her. Somehow, they collapsed every night lately, back to back, too tired for anything else. She had heard of a seven-year slump, but after two years, it didn't feel right. If only he'd find a job that excited him; if only they could make a great sale and triple their money; if only they could move into that amazing Victorian off Bedlam Street in Cold Spring Harbor they had just purchased. It was so beautiful, resting atop an outcropping of rocks, overlooking the crescent-shaped bay. Julie's pencil snapped in two; she hadn't realized she'd been gripping it so tightly.

The phone buzzed, breaking her concentration. Mr. Wilson's curt voice came through the receiver. "Get me the Shapiro file."

"Which Shapiro? Father or son?"

"I was on the phone with Doug Shapiro all morning. That should be enough for you to realize which one I want."

"I…I was working with Dulcie—"

"Don't give me your life story!" The line went dead, and Julie took a long look at her boss's door. She would love to tell him where to put the file, but she got up to retrieve it. Joanne guarded his door like Charon at the gates of hell.

"Shapiro?" Joanne held out a strong hand, her nails painted a deep power red.

"The father. How was I supposed to know?"

"He pays you to know," Joanne snapped as she snatched the file, and then she went into the inner sanctum of Barry Wilson's office.

Dulcie, Joanne's assistant, looked up sympathetically from her desk. "It's not a big deal."

"You would think. Maybe I should add mind reader to my job description."

Dulcie shushed her with a kind smile, her chocolate-brown eyes dancing. Glancing around, she added, "They hear everything here. Be careful. He's in a bad mood today." She took out an energy bar and offered it to Julie, who shook her head no. Dulcie's brown fingers with bright fuchsia nails stripped off the packaging, crumpling the wrapper and shooting it into the basket.

Julie smiled with approval, clapped quietly, and said, "She scores." A frown graced her brow. "He's always in a bad mood. What makes you think today is any different?"

"Well, it's worse than usual." She leaned closer. "It's his wife," she whispered. "I think she's leaving him."

"Oops. That makes three. What's he going to do now?"

Dulcie got up and walked around the desk, discreetly looking around. "I'd watch out. I heard he likes to fish in his own pond, if you know what I mean."

"That's not true. Number one was his college sweetheart, two was a flight attendant, and three—"

"Came from accounting."

"Why didn't I know that?" Julie wondered.

"It was when you met Brad. You weren't aware of too much. It was hard to have a coherent conversation with you."

"Yeah," Julie replied. "Those were the days."

Joanne came out of the office and eyed the two younger girls. "Don't you have anything better to do?" she demanded. They scattered apart, Julie leaving for her desk.

Maybe they would make enough on the sale of this house so that she could leave here and devote herself to their flipping business. But, she thought dreamily, she did love the bones of that house.

CHAPTER TWO

B rad cleared his throat, his eyes tearing from the smell of a dead rodent. Using his shovel, he scooped it up, but its bodily fluids had glued it to the floor. He gagged, ran up the stairs to escape out the front door, and hunkered down on the steps to deeply breathe in the crisp October air. The house was at the end of a long gravel drive at the top of a hill, overlooking the waters of Long Island Sound. The address read Bedlam Street, but it was actually almost a mile from the road, affording the occupants privacy. It was a big house, with clumsy additions added on through the ages and looking to him like a doughy-faced dowager. Sitting on the first step of the porch, he watched the gray waters of the sound, the autumn shades of the trees surrounding the bay like a bowl. Seagulls screeched, diving to pluck small mollusks from the shallow water and then dropping them on the beach to break apart. They protected their bounty, fighting off interlopers to feast on their seafood snack. His stomach rumbled, but he couldn't eat. The musty smell of the basement killed any thought of lunch. His eyes were gritty with filth. This was by far the dirtiest flip they had attempted, and he longed to tell Julie to list it on eBay for a dollar more than they had paid for it, but he knew Julie had a bug about this house. She loved it, and he couldn't understand why. It was old, dilapidated, and a monster of a repair. He'd almost lost his temper this morning when she rapped out fifty things that needed to be done. He didn't need her to remind him; he knew what had to be done. He didn't mind walking away from this project. He trotted to his truck, removed his thermos filled with coffee, took a healthy swig, and spit it into the bushes. It cleared the dust from his palate, and he swallowed a satisfying mouthful. His phone broke the peaceful silence. Glancing at the face, he saw that it was Julie, and he swiped it with a dirty finger to answer.

"What's up?" he asked, his throat gravelly.

"You didn't call me all day," Julie said, a tone of plaintiveness in her voice.

"I didn't know I was expected to report in."

Julie sighed. "Brad, what's wrong? We usually speak a few times a day. Look, day after tomorrow I'll be there to help."

"I don't even know if I want you to help, Jules. This place is disgusting. I just had to peel a decomposing rat off the floor. I don't want you in the place."

"Honey, we are in this together. Look, it was a great price. If it works out well, we'll make enough to buy two houses with the profit. Maybe I can quit my job," she finished in a hopeful whisper.

Brad was silent. It was a long-held dream. He didn't like her boss, the sleazy son of a bitch. He never made eye contact with Brad. But the fact was, they got their medical and 401k there, plus her salary would keep them going until they could turn the flipping into a profitable business. Profitable meant that he could stop taking landscaping jobs in the spring and they would make enough to live off the flips. They had even discussed an income property, but they didn't have enough to tie up their capital in a rental house. Her boss had been instrumental in helping them with their loans. If not for him and the generous terms he negotiated, none of this would have been possible. So far, they had only made enough to pay their bills and move on to the next house. They hadn't accrued anything. Other than the small house they lived in, they had no real equity. They had a ways to go—especially when his truck died and they had to buy a slightly used pickup. The down payment had put a dent in their savings.

"This is worse than the Tate house." Two houses ago, they'd picked up an estate sale. The house hadn't been touched for many years, and they had to rip out everything. They had made next to nothing, and it was one of their less successful ventures because they weren't prepared for the extent of the damage. Julie knew he was reminding her of that fiasco.

"We were rookies then," she pleaded. "We know what we are doing now. The homes on that hill go for the high nines right now. We bought it for nothing."

"That's because it's worth nothing. I don't have time. We only have the container until the end of the week, so I have to finish clearing out the garbage," he snapped. He said a hasty good-bye and slid his phone into his back pocket. He looked up at the house, the sun's rays glinting off the multicolored stained glass window. Hands on hips, he considered the building. It was butt ugly. He laughed, shaking his head as he walked up the front steps again to tackle the lower levels of hell, his new name for the basement of the house.

He went down into the darkness, reaching up to find the string that lit the single lightbulb. He didn't remember turning it off, he thought, as he stumbled into a pile of trash. His shin connected hard with the corner of a metal box, and Brad cursed loudly and fluently. The light flicked on, and he searched the room, his eyes wide. The hanging bulb swayed as though pushed, and Brad turned where he stood, looking for an intruder. Reaching up, he pulled the cord, extinguishing the light, and touched the hot bulb gingerly. Twisting it gently, he quickly determined it was not loose. He relit it, searching the ceiling to see if the connection to the fixture itself was compromised. It must be dicey wires, he reasoned. After all, the house was really old. He wondered how safe the wiring was, making a mental note to recheck all the connections. The light moved gently, painting peculiar shadows on the walls. The room was dim for sure, but a brightness illuminated the dark corners. Brad watched the pools of light speculatively, the hair on the back of his neck rising as the tension grew. Hearing a footstep, he spun, his hand instinctively reaching for a firearm he no longer carried. His breath came in short gasps, and his eyes darted around the room, until he felt the vacuum of emptiness. Something fell, but he took in the nothingness of the space.

There was the sound of metal scraping against metal on the other side of the room. Brad walked closer, gingerly putting his ear against the cool wall. Tapping the surface with his knuckle, he heard the emptiness of the other side. It was a secret room, a walled-up space, he thought with astonishment. He laughed uneasily when the old Edgar Allan Poe story popped into his mind—what was it? "The Tell-Tale Heart." He wondered if he'd find a chained skeleton bolted to the wall. His fingers caressed the surface, looking for an opening. Another thump. Something fell on the hidden side. He banged on the wall, feeling foolish. There was a rumble of sound. Brad shrugged with impatience. Using his shovel as an ax, he hit the wall, breaking plaster, raining dust all over him. With all his might, he hit it again, pulverizing the ancient slat work under the wall to break into a vacant space. Stale air hit him in the face, and he created enough of an opening to slide into the pitch-black area through the rent in the wall. Placing his hands on either side of it, he lowered himself through the opening. The floor of the other side was a good five feet deeper than the basement.

The flashlight in Brad's phone illuminated the cave-like quality of the room. He hugged the wall, knowing he was deep in the ground, below the basement. He held up the light, the breath escaping from his lungs. The room was filled with rows and rows of boxes and crates. They were stacked nine feet high, some broken from the weight. The contents of two containers had spilled out; papers and knickknacks littered the dirt floor. He bent, his fingers going through the rubble to pick up a leather box, its binding cracked. He opened it to find an antique sewing kit, complete with colored thread that hadn't seen the light of day for over 150 years. He shoved at a container lying sideways on the floor, jumping back, his heart racing, when a rat skittered over his booted foot. "Pussy," he muttered, disgusted with himself. His face heated, and he wondered where all this unease was coming from. He had seen things during his four years overseas that would have broken his late mother's heart, but had hardly rocked him. He couldn't understand what unnerved him about this house. Reaching up, he pulled down a box, finding housewares, gloves, all kinds of delicate lacework, table-cloths, dishes, tools—it was a treasure trove of junk, the stuff of everyday life dating back to who knew when.

He pulled out his phone and dialed the trash people, letting them know they had to pick up the filled Dumpster and replace it, and that he needed a larger one for at least another week. He slid out a credit card and read them the number to pay for the additional equipment. Going through this pile was going to add an extra week he really couldn't afford. It meant delaying the repairs, which would result in showing the house later. Brad cursed, knowing that with winter around the corner, they might be stuck with this wreck, paying their contractor loan into the spring. It also meant they couldn't afford to move on to the next house, so he cursed again. He looked at the four walls of the room. He was on the other side of the subbasement. He knocked on the wall, hearing its hollow-ness. Punching a hole through the plaster, he realized he was on the other side of the outside of the house. It was a secret room deep in the bowels of the house, sealed with plaster to be hidden away for perhaps a hundred years or so. He considered for what reason the room might have been walled off. There was a good chance they might find some valuables. Why else would there be a secret room? Perhaps they'd find some things to sell to compensate for the delays. He coughed, his throat clogging from the odor. Something had died in the room. Brad recognized the smell of decay. *Probably a nest of dead rats*, he thought grimly.

Brad eyed the dusty boxes in the corner with distaste, but he knew he had no choice. Pushing them through the narrow opening and then carting them up the rickety staircase, he made a neat pile in the center of the parlor. Cold, damp air seeped in from outside; the salon echoed with emptiness. In the living room, there was a faint musty smell, and a giant rusty watermark stained the carved plaster of the ceiling. It was a huge area, with a scuffed parquet floor, the walls a depressing mahogany paneling. It was so big it probably had doubled as a ballroom. A filthy wooden dado spanned all the walls around the room, empty but for mice droppings. He wondered if these boxes contained all the knickknacks that had decorated it, for which the fussy Victorian era was famous. Flowered wallpaper hung in shreds over the high paneling. Hands on hips, Brad surveyed the exotic wood covering the walls almost to the high ceiling. He walked over to rap on the surface with his knuckle.

Gerald, observing from the doorway, laughed deeply and said, "Knock, knock."

Brad cocked his head, as if he had heard something. "Boo," he whispered to the empty room. They could get a nice few dollars for all this wood. He knew of a place in Connecticut that could probably sell it on consignment. Getting rid of it would certainly lighten up the room a bit. Victorians weren't his thing. He preferred the clean lines of midcentury modern, with organic colors. The walls, painted dark gray and with their oppressive gothic woodwork, were overbearing. He and Julie did not see eye to eye on this style. But, now he had a group of boxes to investigate for anything interesting and worth keeping. He pulled over a builder's paint can to sit on while he sifted through the many boxes.

Most held clothing from the early twentieth century. He damn near had a heart attack after tearing one box open to find a moth-eaten fur wrap. It had six little rodent heads, with twelve glass eyes caught in a permanent look of surprise. "Ugh." Gingerly, he picked it up with his index and thumb and threw it onto the growing pile of refuse. "Are you the guys responsible for all the mouse shit in here?" He laughed. The triangular faces stared at him blankly. He stood, scanned the room for an old towel, and threw it over the faces. "Rest in peace, you little suckers."

"If he throws away my fox stole, you are going to have to kill him," Tessa said.

"Me? Why me? I certainly don't care. I hated that thing on you. It aged you dreadfully," Gerald replied, seating himself on a box. "He really is making a mess here."

"You never even saw me in it. I got it after—"

"Oh, Tessa, I saw you in it."

Tessa ignored him as she stared at Brad. "Look at his shoulders. I could just—"

"You could just not," Gerald corrected. "Not your place. He's married."

"Since when did that matter?" Tessa sniffed. Coughing, she waved her graceful arms before her. "Oh, the dust." She used to be a tall woman; people had called her robust. To Gerald, she was enchanting, with her masses of red-gold hair and mysterious gray eyes. She had porcelain skin with a hint of roses in her full cheeks. He never tired of staring at her—or at her magnificent bosom.

"Cut it out, Tessa, you can't breathe anymore. Stop waving. He doesn't notice you."

"Yet." Tessa looked at Gerald with a faint moue of distaste. He was still here, even after all these years. When was that man going to understand that she wasn't interested in him? He was as boring now as he had been back then. Her narrowed eyes compared her companion's lean form to the vital human stirring up all the dust, as well as her desires, in the parlor. She watched the fabric of Brad's shirt tighten against the muscles of his taut shoulders. He brushed back his bothersome hair that fell against his damp face, the weak sunlight glinting off the sweat of his burnished forearms. Shivering with need, she licked her lips and exhaled deeply, turning into smoke to envelop Brad.

Brad stood still, his features frozen. He looked around the room, cocking his head. What was that? Bands tightened around his chest, and for a minute his breathing became labored. He thought he must have pulled a muscle carrying up that last box. Stretching, he stood to spread his arms wide, trying to get air into his lungs, but he found it difficult to breathe. He leaned forward, attempting to relieve the pressure. Maybe he was having a heart attack. His dad had died of heart disease. Sweat beaded his brow, and his hair slipped out of its ponytail to curtain his wet face.

"Stop it. You're choking him." Gerald swirled around her.

"But he feels so good," Tessa purred, relishing the feel of human contact. "A few minutes ago, you were trying to scare him into leaving."

"A few minutes ago, he was sweeping up my newspapers. He's a nuisance, but I don't want to hurt him." He watched her spirit glow as she sucked the strength from the young man. Tessa was intrigued, and that was bothersome. This one was almost too handsome, and that could turn into a problem.

The room dimmed; as his sight narrowed to a pinprick, Brad thought for sure he was going to pass out.

"He's swooning." Strong arms grabbed Tessa, forcing her to let go. She inflated, her eyes glowing red as she reared up in hatred.

"Leave me alone, Gerald. You never let me have any fun."

"You were killing him, darling. I can't let you hurt them," he said as she flew up the chimney in a fury. "You don't want the Sentinels to interfere, do you?" he called after her ominously. His voice echoed back to him. He chuckled, his rakish face smiling. He circled the interloper in a fine gray mist.

"Handsome is as handsome does," he said, admitting with a shake of his head that this was a rare specimen of male perfection. *Why couldn't he be fifty and bald?* he speculated. This was going to be a problem. Tessa was attracted to this human, and he could see why. Materializing above the mortal, Gerald watched him struggle for air, hating the fact that he knew this man was vital and alive. Gerald was tired of being stuck here in this sort of limbo, waiting for Tessa. He really should just leave, he thought, as he dissolved into yellow smoke to follow Tessa up the chimney.

The howling wind in the fireplace flue was the first thing Brad noticed as his breathing returned to normal. Doubled over, the crushing weight had disappeared with the same haste as it began. Whatever it was, he was fine now. *No more burritos for breakfast*, he thought. He was going back to egg whites. Clearing his throat, he shook his head; his pulse slowed to normal, and he decided he was just winded. What else could it be? He rested his hand on the dark wood mantel, feeling a strange vibration in its surface. *This was getting too weird*, he thought. He had to shake off the feelings of doom and gloom. He had work to do, and it wasn't going to get done by itself. The longer they took with the flip, the more his wife would get attached to it. The sky was darker, rain was coming on, and he would have liked to finish tomorrow, but knew he had another good hour of work left. Saturday would be easier with the two of them going through the mountains of refuse. Julie would be able to tell whether some of this junk was valuable.

He lit the flimsy chandelier with its tulip glass shades. Its light flickered and wavered, bathing the room in a buttery hue. Brad shivered a bit, then sat down on the can to start sorting through another of the boxes. He and Julie had figured all the valuables had been stripped by the more recent occupants, but he had found a pretty good haul in the undisturbed hole. Forty-five minutes later, he had more piles than he could count: clothes, letters, books, any papers he found interesting, a tidy pile of old money, perfume bottles, canes, old lace-up shoes, parasols, and a growing stack of paintings. He picked up an old glass lampshade covered with grime. Brushing dirt from the mosaic pattern of the glass, his breath caught in his throat when the trapped colors were freed to reflect in patterns on the wall. He held it up to the late sunlight streaming in the bare window and spun it slowly, watching the reds, blues, greens, and yellows paint the dull room with vibrancy. It was like spring had entered hell, he thought with a wry grin. Might be valuable. He gingerly placed it in an empty box to take home. His eyes smarted from the dust, and as much as he'd wanted to go through the rest of the house, his back was aching. This work was filthy.

Brad had agreed to this business because he hated driving the limo. After being in Afghanistan, chauffeuring the rich and spoiled seemed superfluous. It was hard to keep his mouth shut when they demanded he speed up to risk a ticket because they were running late. Some paid him just to walk their dog. It was stupid work. This was much more satisfying. He had worked with his father around the house when he was a kid, so most of the minor repairs were easy. Brad had liked the feeling of pride when he handed over the keys to the young couple who'd bought the flip they finished last month. It was a two-bedroom Cape, an easy fixer-upper they bought at foreclosure for less than $40,000. Twenty thousand went toward insulation, a new kitchen, one new bath, and a fresh coat of paint. They did it in the industrial style, all lean lines, and it sold for over $180,000. They made a tidy profit, their biggest, and Julie had spotted this monstrosity on the way home. Why, he thought to himself, did he choose to take the long way home? Normally, they went on the highway, but that night he took the scenic route, and Julie had screeched for him to stop when she saw the for-sale sign swinging in the breeze.

"Oh…my…God! I love this place." She urged him to go up the winding driveway. It was steep and narrow, made more for horses and carriages. They got to the top of the hill, and Julie leaped out of the car.

"Jules, stop!" he called to his five-foot-nothing wife as she casually jumped the short iron fence. "You can't go—"

"Come on. This place is amazing." She waded through the overgrown yard and got up on the porch to peer through a window.

It was big, a genuine Victorian, with dirty white shingles and a dilapidated porch that wrapped around the house, supported by posts decorated with gingerbread woodwork at the top. He admitted to himself, it did have a certain charm, if you liked fussy details.

"It's Second Empire," his wife informed him, looking at the flat-topped mansard roof. "Oh, it has a cupola."

"A what?" he asked.

She pointed to an onion-shaped blob on the top of a tower, its gold paint tarnished and peeling off in large strips.

"It's ugly," he told her plainly.

"I think we'll go gray and white with red accents." Julie ignored him as she stared into the gloom of the interior through the wavy glass. "Look at the size of that entry, Brad," she whispered in awe, "the staircase looks like it's never been touched."

"Yeah, Julie, I don't think anything's been touched here. Besides, we're trespassing. It's probably over our budget." Brad only saw mountains of work. "The pipes would have to be pulled out. They're probably lead. Look, Jules." He pressed his work boot down on the warped wood. "The whole place is rotted. This will be too hard for us." He scanned the dilapidated roof, slates broken and missing in spots. The shingles sagged in the center portion of the house. "It looks like the Addams family lived here," he told her wryly, but he knew her mind was made up. "Lurch?" He cupped a hand to his face and called loudly, "Hey, buddy. Lurch. Trick or treat."

Julie nodded absently and, smiling with the determination of a Sherman tank, pulled out her phone. "Please," she pleaded. "Maybe it's a great buy and we'll make a ton. I mean, just look at this place." She held up her arm expansively. It was at least three stories, with a widow's walk facing the calm waters of Cold Spring Harbor. It was nestled in a tangle of overgrown foliage, roots breaking through the floorboards of the porch. The house had a round tower on the side, shaped like a witch's hat. He silently counted the windows. There were forty just on the side he could see. It was too much, he knew—way beyond their capabilities as flippers—but he knew her mind was made up.

Brad shrugged, turning away as Julie punched in the Realtor's number. He didn't see her green eyes light up, but he heard her squeal with delight at the price. Three weeks and a construction loan later, they were the proud owners of Bedlam House, built in 1859 and owned by one of the prominent families of Cold Spring Harbor. It was named for the street near which it was built. Bedlam Street was the main artery of the tiny harbor town, which was now a picturesque village filled with quaint shops. The house was built by Frank Hemmings, a land and railroad baron, and inherited by his daughter after he died. Over the years, it had housed one of the secretaries of Teddy Roosevelt when he was president, a World War I fighter pilot now buried in the fields of France, and a sinister spinster. It had never left the Hemmings family until the late seventies, when the last descendant died, alone and childless. It was a reformatory for about twenty years until funding stopped. It later had a stint as a failed bed-and-breakfast for a New York minute. Foreclosed by a bank that didn't want it, it was abandoned, deserted and run-down, filled with mice and who knew what else. Lastly, it had been a known hideout for crack addicts until the new sheriff was elected.

It was for sale for $15,000, and Brad understood that Julie could not pass that up. The acre and a half it sat on was worth so much more. The town just wanted someone to rehabilitate it. What Brad didn't understand was why, at that price, none of the local premier real estate brokers or contractors had bought it for demolition. It was an eyesore to him—dirty, smelly, old, and decayed. He didn't like this project and saw this investment as a money pit. But, they were committed. They didn't have the funds for anything more than a bare-bones renovation, with him doing the bulk of the work.

Brad remembered the day they got the keys and went in for an inspection. He had to admit there was a faded grandeur about the place. The entry was huge, with a winding spiderweb of a staircase that seemed to go on forever. It had a cold stone floor; it reminded him of an indoor porch. A stained glass window dominated the large first landing. It was a depiction of Joan of Arc, with masses of blond hair stuck under her pointed helmet. She had a doll-like face, blue eyes, and a voluptuous body. A white horse stood docilely at her side. He stared dumbfounded at the interpretation of the French saint.

"What were they thinking? We should rip that out," he told Julie.

"No way." She raced up the stairs to examine it closer. "It was a Victorian perception of what Joan looked like.

"Joan of Arc is rolling in her grave at this depiction."

"She was burned at the stake," Julie informed him.

"Well then, she's spinning like a gyro. Man, that's horrible, Jules."

"It's authentic to the time period."

"Gives me the creeps. No wonder all they thought about was death."

"What are you talking about?" Julie turned to face him.

"The Victorians created most of today's funeral customs. They loved nothing more than decorating cemeteries with all those statues and stuff. Must have come from sitting in depressing places like this."

"Are you kidding me? This place is a diamond in the rough. Look at that fireplace." She ran down the stairs and into the main salon, where a giant black wood mantel filled with carved animal heads took up almost a whole wall. It had a many-shelved étagère surrounding it.

"Cheerful," he smirked, his white teeth bright in his tanned face.

"It is a bit over the top, but it's so Victorian. Look at the paneling."

"Dark," Brad commented grimly.

"I think it's beautiful." Julie hugged him. "Work your magic, Brad, and we'll make this into a showplace."

Brad did not like the speculative gleam in his wife's eye. He caressed her cheek and kissed her on the lips, smiling when he knew he had her full attention. "This is just another flip, Jules."

"What?" She looked like a startled kitten, knowing that somehow he was reading her thoughts. "You know, Brad, we could turn it into a bed-and-breakfast again."

Julie's mind was like a hamster on a wheel, always running—thinking of new ways to make money. She could be harebrained; some of her ideas were just plain dumb. Brad never minded telling her, either. They had some pretty big fights, but the make-up sex made it all worthwhile, he thought with a smile. Somehow it was always sweeter when she was the victor, so he let her think she won more times than not. However, this was not one of those times.

"I don't think so, Jules. We can't afford to carry both our mortgage and the construction loan."

"We could consolidate and move in here…," she said, her voice trailing off as she caressed the coffered mahogany paneling.

"Sure, and we'll shower at the gas station in town?"

"Think about it?"

"I did, and I'm not anymore."

"Any more what?" she asked hopefully.

"Thinking about it."

Now Brad stood in an endless pile of filth, two days into the cleanup. Wearily, he packed his tool belt away, his chest still smarting from the strange pressure he'd just experienced. "We'll make this into a showplace," he said sarcastically to himself. He set the paint can on a pile of papers to prevent them from moving. Flipping through the stack of paintings, he pulled out four that looked like they might be worth something. One was of the house in better days. A smile graced his lips as he thought Julie was right—it had the bones for beauty, but time and circumstances had not been kind to the old house.

He paused at the portrait of a woman in nineteenth-century clothing, her hair up in a tasteful chignon, her wistful smile catching his eye. She was not exactly beautiful by today's standards, with her strong jaw and longish nose. But there was something special about her. Using a rag, he dusted off the filthy frame. Nails caressed the back of his neck, and he whipped around, rattled, his eyes wild. He knew what he felt, and his body had reacted, he thought uncomfortably, adjusting himself. Flames danced down his arm, goose bumps appearing. His breath harsh in his chest, he used the filthy rag to brush away imagined insects. Insects? he thought wildly. What kind of insects could affect him like that? His lips prickled as though Julie's sweet breath were upon them. He backed away from the pressure of a hand on the center of his chest, until his back touched the ratty wallpaper that hung in strands from the top of the walls. Whispers echoed in his ears, a cold fog surrounding him, and he heard feminine laughter. He looked out the window, wondering where the sound was coming from, dismissing it as a passing car.

Tessa leaned against the warmth of a vital human, her lips caressing, her tongue licking him. Wrapping her arms around him, she inhaled his male scent, her eyes dreamy. She pressed into him, sliding her legs against the hardness of Brad, hooking hers around his lean legs. Smiling, she heard his breath catch, then closed her eyes and covered his mouth with her own, when a roar deafened the room, a claw grabbing her by the neck to shake her like a wet puppy and throw her violently against the wall.

"Get out of my house!" Tessa screamed at the black shadow hovering between the two of them, unseen by the human. It laughed, mocking her, becoming a solid wall as she rose to go through it. It was as dense as obsidian, cutting her vaporous form into tiny splinters to break apart like shattered ice. Tessa reformed, angrily backing out of the room, watching the black cloud grow to encompass the entire space, including the human. She bared her teeth, words failing her, and left in search of Gerald. The thing had come back, and she was not happy.

Brad watched in amazement as the floor lit up with scattered dots of light, like sprinkled raindrops. They reminded him of the tiny tea lights he had used to propose to Julie, but vanished seconds later, leaving him to wonder if he had imagined the whole thing. There was a heaviness weighing him down, pinning him to the wall like a butterfly specimen. His ears rang as though a gun had gone off. He rolled his neck, Afghanistan coming back to him in a rush. Sweating, he slid down the wall, wondering if PTSD had finally gotten to him.

A coldness invaded the room. Brad squinted at the descending sun, wondering why its bright rays failed to penetrate the gloomy space. Cocking his head, he thought it strange, as the room faced the west and should be filled with warm light, yet there was an oppressive pall that smothered the place. His phone rang, breaking the silence, and he slipped it out of his back pocket.

"Hi, honey." Julie's voice filled the vacuum of the room.

"Yeah," Brad said tonelessly, unaccountably irritated by her happy greeting.

"You OK?" Julie asked.

"Great," he replied curtly.

"I just left the office. I'll be home in forty-five." She paused. "Do you want to pick up Chinese food?"

"I'm filthy. Don't you have anything in the house?" He stood, growing more impatient with his wife. He could feel the agitation in the pit of his stomach and couldn't prevent the resentment from showing. His voice welled with anger. "I thought we said we were going to watch the spending, Julie. This flip is going to cost a fortune."

Julie held the phone away from her ear, sighing. He was so mad. Over what, dinner? "Really? When was I supposed to get the groceries, during my lunch break?" she retorted, her voice rising. Her neck had turned red. "Look, Brad, I—"

"Never mind." Her husband cut her off. "I'm not even hungry. I'll see you later." He hung up without letting her answer.

CHAPTER THREE

Julie was pissed. He was so angry lately. Ever since they purchased this house, the light had left his eyes. He had been so easygoing about everything. That's what had drawn her to him in the first place. Brad was different from all her other boyfriends. He was kind, patient, sweet, and fun to be around. Nothing ever rocked his world. She had been attracted to him for all the obvious reasons. He had the most perfect face; tanned, with lovely gray eyes. He had that boyish surfer look; his long brown hair was streaked by the sun, and he had the toned body of an athlete. Never overdressed, he filled out jeans and a work shirt like an underwear model. Her father never liked him, unhappy with his lack of a career, yet Julie just didn't care. She had loved him from the first time he ran to her side of the car and opened the door, helping her out like she was a porcelain doll. She punched in his number again, wanting to finish what they started, but canceled the call, thinking he would get home first, shower, and perhaps cool down enough for them to have an adult conversation. She called her sister Heather instead.

"Hi, Julie. Everything OK?"

"Do you have a minute?"

"Barely. I'm picking up Cooper at soccer and then I have to get Lainey from the orthodontist. I have a PTA meeting at eight, and Jack just called and is going to be late. What's up, sweetie?"

Julie sighed. "I don't get it...we were cruising along. Everything was great, you know." Julie paused.

"What? Did you have a fight?"

"Nooo, not precisely. I'm not even sure if there is a problem. I mean, well, there is...I mean, like a problem."

"Julie, get to the point. I don't have much time. Are you having a problem with money? Talk, Jules. Is it in the bedroom?"

"Well, I'm not having a problem, but lately he doesn't want to do anything. It's like he can't stand me."

"Oh, honey. That happens to everyone. One day it's rainbows and puppy dogs and then...well, they just get over it. Jules, did anything happen?"

"No! I mean everything was moving along fine. We sold the Cape, made some nice money." Julie went silent, then continued, "It's since we bought this new house."

"The old Hemmings place? Hi, Cooper. Throw your stuff in the back."

Julie heard her nephew enter the car, and her sister switched off her speakerphone.

"Coop's in the car, so I won't be able to say much. Look, they all go through stages, Jules. That place was a sty. Is he working hard there?"

"He got angry when I asked him to pick up some dinner. I don't remember the last time he, you know—"

"You asked him to pick up dinner? Isn't today his birthday?"

"Shit. I forgot." Julie was silent for a moment. "I am working full time, too, if you haven't noticed. This is hard, Heather."

"I know, it sucks. But what are the choices? You have to make enough to survive today. It's never enough. Cooper! Stop hitting the back of my seat. Look, I've got to go. Make him a home-cooked dinner and then take matters into your own hands. You know what I mean?"

"Thanks, sis." Julie hung up, resentful but willing to try what her sister suggested. Brad and she weren't like her sister and her husband. She thought they had a relationship built on friendship and an equality that didn't need the games others needed to play. Brad liked her aggressiveness, treating her as a partner first, and as a woman second. She loved that about him.

Julie got into her small car parked at the train station. Instead of going home, she pulled into the supermarket and bought a roasted chicken, mashed potatoes, and a vegetable in the deli section. It was as close to a home-cooked meal as she could put together on such short notice. Then she ran into the local bakery to buy the most decadent chocolate cake it had.

CHAPTER FOUR

B rad pulled his truck into the carport, got out, and opened the rear door to take out the paintings he had brought home. He lugged them one by one into their small ranch house and rested them against the couch in the shabby living room. He went back for the lampshade, placing the box on the coffee table. All the furniture was secondhand—not that he minded, but he knew Julie did. They'd bought this tiny house just before the wedding. It was little more than an apartment on a slab, with a small utility kitchen, a living room with a cozy fireplace, and three tiny bedrooms that looked more like closets with windows. The bathroom was still vomit-green, circa 1978, and the harvest-gold kitchen appliances were so old they had started looking trendy. He had ripped out the shag carpet himself and surprised Julie by polishing the blond wooden floor, then covering it with a Berber area rug that they had made love on in front of a roaring fire. He stopped and stared at the spot where he had knocked over a glass of wine during that evening. Though the rug was new, Julie hadn't minded. She'd giggled and said she'd never be able to look at the rug without thinking of them humping away, throwing both caution and wine to the wind. A smile split his face, his even teeth gleaming, the depression that sat heavily on him all day dissipating.

He stripped quickly, stepped into the shower, and let the needles of hot water pierce through the dirt coating his skin.

Julie entered the house and put the food on the bridge table they were currently using in the dining room. The fourth leg wobbled; it always looked ready to collapse. Brad promised her it was sound. Sliding out of her shoes, she used a toe to gently press it outward, until satisfied that it wouldn't fall.

"Brad," she called, removing her coat and hanging it on a hook in the dim entry by the door. "Brad?" She heard the water running in the bathroom. Quickly, she slipped off her shirt and the rest of her clothes, silently opening the door to the pint-sized bathroom. Condensation covered the mirror; it was like walking into a cloud. Angling the shower curtain, she slid in and put her arms around the slippery form of her husband and his taut belly. He was sudsy. She pressed her nose against his firm shoulder, inhaling his scent, and brought her entire body in contact with his. She heard his sigh, but she wasn't sure if it was of contentment or despair.

"Happy birthday," she whispered, taking him into her hand and sliding down the length of him. This time she knew the sigh was of contentment.

Brad stopped, closing his eyes and caressing her smooth arms with his soapy hands. Julie kissed his back and then placed her cheek flush with his slick skin. She heard him rumble, "Jules." He turned to embrace her, and they lost themselves to the heat, water, and the glorious sensations of skin against skin. Dinner didn't seem to matter after all.

They stumbled out of the shower, spent, replete, and ready for more on their king-size bed. The room was so small, it was literally wall-to-wall mattress. They had no room for a dresser or nightstands. A television hung on the wall.

Much later, Julie mumbled, "Thank goodness for flat screens." She was lying in Brad's arms, the down comforter twisted around them.

"What?" He looked down at her.

"The TV." She gestured at the screen against the wall.

"You want to watch something?" he asked incredulously.

"No." She turned to give him a long kiss on his lips. He put his arms around her slim back and pulled her against him, their bodies fitting tightly together. "I was just wondering where we would have put a television if we couldn't hang it up."

"I never had one in my room. This is a luxury."

Julie looked up at him, her fingers dancing around his lips. Brad caught them, nipping them gently. She brushed the hair from his face. She opened her mouth to complain about the room, but decided not to ruin the mood. "Tell me about the house today."

Brad's slate-gray eyes darkened for a moment.

"What? Were there any problems?"

Brad clicked his tongue. "It's a mess. Too much dust. Too much wind."

"Wind?" Julie asked, only to be cut off by Brad's lips.

He rolled her over and moved down her body, kissing her softly. Julie opened her arms and closed her eyes. She wanted to ask another question, but it fluttered out of her head like an escaping butterfly.

Hours later, they sat with the chicken between them, ripped into manageable parts. They ate it right out of the box.

"You want potatoes?" Julie asked, her mouth full.

Brad wiped a bit of food from the corner of her mouth. "Nope. This is enough."

She was wearing his T-shirt and nothing else. Greasy napkins littered the cover. Brad held up oily hands, looking for another napkin, laughing at Julie's squeal when he motioned that he was going to wipe his hands on the white comforter.

"I saw some artwork and a box in the living room."

"There're a few things worth taking to Sal's." Sal was an antique dealer who directed them with their finds. He paid them fairly and, when it was warranted, arranged for things to be brought to auctions. Julie cocked her head. Brad smiled at her. "I found mounds of boxes in a sealed-off room in the cellar."

"Spooky." Julie rolled her eyes.

"You don't know the half of it," Brad mumbled.

"What?" Julie asked, her fingers shredding a chicken wing.

"Nothing. It's just going to take some extra time to go through all the boxes. I found a sampler." He paused. "It looks to be early, you know, from, like, the eighteen hundreds."

"Folk art." Julie nodded. "I watch *Antiques Roadshow*, too. What did it say?"

Brad laughed at her. "Not sure. Something like 'Home is where the heart is,' I think. Looks homemade, like a kid did it. Then there was a landscape, dark with lots of greens."

"Could be a Hudson River School painting."

"I don't think so. It looks like a painting of the house. Probably a local artist."

"Was there a name?"

Brad nodded.

"Good. I'll google the name tomorrow. What else?" She burped delicately, and Brad laughed out loud.

"There's a portrait, probably a Hemmings ancestor. Then I found a print—could be Manet."

"Framed?" she questioned.

"Impressively. All rococo and gold leaf." Brad took a swig from a pony-neck bottle of Samuel Adams Summer Ale. It was icy-cold, the way he liked it.

"Eclectic." Julie smiled. "That could generate some nice income if it's real. The frames alone could bring us a few dollars. If it's a Manet, it would be nice to keep."

"To hang in this dump? I think not. Where are you going?" Brad called to her as she skittered out of the room, the bottom of her tight little ass exposed underneath his shirt. "It's probably just a copy anyway. I didn't see any numbers."

"I'm sure everything was culled through when the bed-and-breakfast people bought the house." Her voice came from the kitchen.

"I don't know. The basement is a regular time capsule. I did find the false wall and the room filled with boxes. I've barely scratched the surface on separating the things in there. I didn't even have a chance to get into the attic."

Julie walked into the room with the biggest chocolate cake he'd ever seen. Thirty-six lit candles decorated the top, illuminating her rosy cheeks. "Do you want me to sing?" she asked with a smile.

"Only if you want to invite raccoons." Brad made room for her on the bed.

"Make a wish," Julie told him with excited eyes.

"I got it already." Brad kissed her. "But I'll make another." He wriggled his eyebrows.

"I can make the wish for you," she offered hopefully, her green eyes lit with appeal. Julie never gave up once she had an idea in her pretty little head.

Brad was too tired to humor her tonight. "We are not keeping it, Jules. Maybe the next one."

Julie pouted, but turned it into a smile, not wanting to risk the cold war again. This was nicer, more like old times.

Without taking his eyes off her, he blew out the candles gently. "Where are the forks?"

"We don't need no forks!" she told him playfully, digging her fingers into the cake and putting it into his mouth.

Brad smiled, sucking on her fingers, his eyes rolling with pleasure. Julie squealed when he returned the favor. They fed each other, kissed, and ate some more. Soon their faces were smeared with chocolate, crumbs everywhere.

"Oh, this is a mess." Julie stood, brushed brown bits off the white comforter, and watched them leave tiny smears. For the first time, she couldn't get herself to care about it. "By the way, don't go into the attic while you're alone. Wait till Saturday or when Willy is with you," Julie warned him. "You remember what happened the last time."

Brad had climbed into the attic of their last flip and had fallen out, breaking his leg. Without Willy's help, they couldn't have finished the house. Brad had worn a cast for weeks, and even now she knew his leg pained him.

Willy was an army buddy who helped with the repair jobs. An out-of-work vet, he was willing to wait until they sold the house to get paid. They always gave him a small percentage. There was nothing the man couldn't or wouldn't do.

"Time is money, baby. We have to move this one, and Willy can't come until next week. He went to Charleston to visit his mom." Brad lay back, his face distant. His eyes narrowed, and Julie wondered what he was thinking about. His lips turned down, and his fist absently tapped against the counterpane.

Julie contemplated the wrecked cake in the box. "Are you still mad?"

"I'm not mad, Jules." Brad pushed her hair behind her ear and lifted her chin so their eyes met. "This is a big house." He placed his finger over her lips when she started to interrupt him. "We can't keep it. Please, let's just move it quickly." He shivered, goose bumps pebbling the bare expanse of his chest. "It gives me the creeps." He pulled her forward to kiss her lips. "There'll be other houses."

CHAPTER FIVE

Julie filled her travel mug and was rushing to get her satchel organized when Brad walked into the room.

His hair hung damply over his forehead, his sleepy eyes dominant in his tanned face. He smiled, and for a moment, her breath caught at the beauty of him. Julie longed to throw her keys in the disposal, forget about her job, and stay home to work with her husband all day.

"I'm meeting with the foundation people today. I think they should be able to raise the sagging floor in the subbasement," Brad told her as he stretched. He reached for his mug to prepare a cup of coffee. Eyeing his wife, he said, "Earth to Julie…Jules…you paying attention?"

Julie stared at him, not comprehending, struck by his perfection. His flannel shirt was open, the golden hairs on his chiseled chest glinting. Julie shook her head. "Got it. Foundation today. Please stay out of the attic, Brad."

"I have to get the work done."

"When is Willy returning?" Julie leaned against the counter in their kitchen and looked at him over the rim of her aluminum mug.

Brad hopped up onto the patterned Formica counter. It was chipped in so many places. The border hung half off. Brad pounded it with his fist until the tacky glue stuck.

Julie sighed. "I hate this place."

Brad pushed the lid down on the coffeemaker, touched the button, and watched as his mug filled. "It's a lot nicer than what I lived in as a kid."

"We could just do the counter. I'm not suggesting new cabinets."

Brad shook his head. "I don't want to stay here forever. It's just a stopover."

She contemplated the golden oak cabinets, the warped doors—the wood was so faded by time, the old varnish had turned them orange. He didn't care about his surroundings, but she did. Julie loved to live among elegant and stylish things. While she appreciated that Brad had polished the wooden floors, she longed to rip out the fixtures and make an up-to-date metro galley kitchen.

"We don't have to make double payments on the mortgage," Julie appealed to him. "We could slow it down and make this place more habitable."

"Someone's got to decide which shithole gets first dibs. Hold on, Julie. Don't get angry. I didn't pick the Hemmings house." Brad slid off the counter to approach his wife. "I would have taken a rest after the Cape and put in some time here, but you wanted that run-down pile of crap." He shivered.

"What?" She walked into his embrace, feeling his tremors.

"I don't like that house."

"It was a good buy. We could flip this one for less money and live there for a bit. Think about it. We could make an income renting out the rooms. There must be fifteen bedrooms there. That way, we could fix it slowly."

"There're twelve. If you're complaining about the kitchen here, the one at the Hemmings house is prehistoric. Nah." He tipped her face up to meet his, kissing the tip of her upturned nose. "Willy's going to be here next week. I'm pushing to get it done. Just forget about that wreck. Once we sell it, we can spackle this one a bit, put it up for sale, and move to the next one."

Brad kissed the light skin at the base of Julie's neck where her pulse thrummed, smiling at the purr coming from his wife's throat.

"You are doing that on purpose to distract me."

"Guilty." He kissed her fully on the lips.

"You're going to make me late for work again."

"Guilty again."

Julie slid her hands under his shirt, feeling the smooth flesh, the ripples of sculpted muscle wrapped around his lean flanks. He pinned her against the rickety table, her legs anchoring him. Leaning over her, he slid his palm between her legs, touching her in such a way that the condition of the countertop quickly became a distant memory.

An hour later, they found themselves back in the kitchen, satisfied smiles shared between them.

She rubbed at an old brown cigarette burn in the countertop made by some long-ago resident.

"You're going to rip it," Brad warned.

"Maybe it would look better."

"Don't start that now, Julie." Brad shook his head. "Let's finish Hemmings first."

Julie considered the ancient blackened burn. "Do you think a house holds the energy of its inhabitants?"

"That's weird; where's it coming from?"

Julie pointed to the burn. "Someone did this, marked the house. Does it sort of make it his?"

"The woman who made that burn is living in the Del Boca Vista retirement community in Tampa. She has about as much connection to this house as the lawyer who handled the closing."

Julie swallowed. "Listen, think about it. She made a mark here; does it make it hers? Does a part of her stay here forever, like a footprint or a fingerprint?"

"You're a nut, Jules. I've got to go."

CHAPTER SIX

"Well, was it good?" Heather asked Julie over the phone.

"It's always good. It just hasn't been frequent enough."

"Welcome to married life," her sister complained. "Wait till you have kids. You'll have to live on memories."

Julie laughed so hard, it echoed back into the receiver.

"You won't be laughing when it happens to you," Heather warned. "I have an appointment with Cooper's teacher in an hour. He's failing math, and we have to think about our *options*. I'm glad the two of you talked."

"Believe me, there was no talking going on."

"Lucky you," Heather stated.

"He wants to sell the Hemmings house, and I want to move into it. Don't you think it would make a great B-and-B?"

Her sister was silent for a moment. "Marriage is all about compromise. Julie, you can't push a guy like Brad around. He's not your lackey."

"Lackey, are you kidding me? Just because I want to better our life, I get a bum rap. If I were a guy, everybody would say I was ambitious. When you're a woman, you're labeled a bitch if you want to get ahead." Julie snorted. "Anyway, where is the compromise? We both want to make money, so I don't know what all the fuss is about. It's like he's scared of the house."

"Brad?" her sister scoffed. "Brad's not afraid of anything. I've never met a braver guy. He married you, after all."

"Screw you, Heather. I'm a prize." Julie laughed.

"Of course you are, honey. Men get like that. Scared. Sometimes they feel like they're losing control."

"What are you talking about?"

"Think about it, Jules. He does most of the flip himself. I know what's his name—"

"Willy."

"Willy helps, but the whole thing sits on his shoulders. Your success or failure depends mostly on him. That's a lot of responsibility. Sounds to me like Brad just wants to make sure you stay on track and don't get overwhelmed."

"I don't know," Julie replied skeptically.

"No, listen, I only have a minute or so before I have to hang up. Sounds to me like Brad wants to take smaller risks and not get stalled by a project that may be too big for him. Life goes fast, really fast, Jules. First we were dating, then married, and now I'm holding on to the tail end of my thirties with my fingernails. Jack turned forty last year! That's middle age, if we are lucky enough to get to eighty."

"Oh, stop it," Julie laughed. "You have years and years."

"Cooper is going to middle school next year. Lainey, the year after that. Soon they'll be driving. It goes fast. You know Mom always said that the days drag, but the years fly."

"I can't believe she's gone five years already."

"See what I mean? Don't waste time on stupid stuff, Julie. Don't fight with him over nonsense. In the end, it's all bullshit. Nothing matters."

"OK, OK, I hear you. You're creeping me out. You are only six years older than me, and you're talking like you're in AARP."

"Oh, I can't believe this!" Heather said with disgust. "Coop missed the bus. I have to take him to school. I said I'm coming! Call you later, but I mean it. Brad's a great guy. Don't fuss over the nonsense."

Julie clicked off her phone. The train would be there any minute. She slid out of her car and climbed the steep steps to wait by the track. It was still warm, with fall just around the corner. A breeze picked up, and she was sorry she hadn't taken her pashmina wrap to wear over her blazer. It was always so stuffy on the train that she never liked to overdress. She leaned close to a big poster on the platform, trying to duck out of the wind. Turning, she studied the woman staring back at her from the picture. She had a familiar face, but Julie couldn't quite place her. She was short, with white hair in the front of her short hairstyle, black in the rear. She reminded Julie of Cruella de Vil. Julie backed up a bit to see the advertisement. "Georgia Oaken—Resident Medium," the black lettering proclaimed. "Tuesday 9 PM on the Ghost Network."

She remembered now; this woman had her own program where she communicated with the dead. *I wonder how well she communicates with the living*, Julie thought. Maybe she should hire her to help her communicate with Brad better. Julie grinned. The train chugged into the station, the whistle announcing its presence. Julie slipped through an open door, her gaze glued to the poster of the psychic as the train pulled out of town.

CHAPTER SEVEN

B rad cursed and hit the top of the steering wheel with his fist; he'd forgotten to tell Julie about the Tiffany-style lampshade. He had a feeling it was worth a few bucks. He loaded it back into the truck along with the paintings. He would try to swing by Sal's and move it quickly. Maybe he would sell it and surprise Julie by putting the proceeds toward a new counter in their kitchen. He pressed a button on the steering wheel and said, "Telephone, Sal, cell."

The disembodied voice of Siri repeated the information, and three rings later, Sal's gravelly voice filled his truck.

"Sal, it's Brad. How are you?"

"Crazy busy. I have an auction planned for Saturday. You got something?" he asked hopefully. "I need filler."

"I got a bunch of stuff. We bought the Hemmings place."

"Hmm, Bedlam House, that dive. You found anything in there?" Sal inquired.

"Paintings, boxes of Victorian crap."

"Any silver?"

Brad thought for a moment. "Nah. I did see some old colored glass jars with little silver handles."

"What colors?"

"Two blues and a rose one. The rose one might be cracked, though."

"Bonbon jars. Doesn't matter. The blue ones are the more valuable. Red is more common. I can get about a buck or a buck-fifty for them. I'll give you forty apiece."

"Make it fifty. I have a few paintings. I have to look up the artists." Brad paused. "There's a fur wrap."

"Take it to a secondhand store. Fur's not politically correct right now."

"It has, like, six faces on it." Brad shuddered.

"Yuck, I hate those things. Forget about it," Sal said, his Brooklyn accent evident. "I can't move them. There's a little store in Huntington that sells old clothes. I would just give it to them."

"Give it to your new girlfriend—what's her name?" Brad offered.

"Molly. She wouldn't be caught dead in one of those. Anyway, she's more of a bohemian."

"I thought she was a Realtor."

"Hah! Funny." Sal laughed.

"How much for a…what's the name? Yeah, a Tiffany lampshade?"

"What's it look like?" Sal asked.

"I don't know…like an upside-down salad bowl. Little bits of colored glass—"

"Whoa!" Sal interrupted. "The shade or the whole lamp?"

"Just a shade," Brad told him.

"That sucks. It's better with the lamp. What makes you think it's Tiffany?"

"It's the tiny glass mosaics. That's Tiffany, right?" Brad asked.

"Well, there're a lot of fakes out there. What kind of pattern?" Sal paused. "If it's genuine, we could be talking six figures."

Brad stepped on the brake; the truck stopped short. "Seriously?"

"Seriously. Is it a floral?"

"You mean like a flower design? Yeah, lots of flowers."

"Look for a stamp with a date or the name on the iron part. The early shades are really valuable. See if it has a signature. If you find one, it could mean Louis Comfort might have made it himself."

"Who?"

"Louis Comfort Tiffany. That would be golden. Look for that name. And tap on it lightly," Sal advised.

"Why?"

"If it rattles a bit, it could mean it's genuine. When they're old, the solder holding it together shrinks so the glass doesn't fit tightly. Sometimes they make a noise. Don't be too rough with it!"

"Could you sell it?" Brad's hope was rising.

"Does McDonald's have golden arches?" Sal laughed. "Bring it in before you break it, you clumsy oaf, and I'll get it in Saturday's auction."

"No problem. Sal?"

"Yep?"

"Let's keep this between us. I want to surprise Julie. I'll be by later today."

"Got it."

Brad pulled into the broken driveway, his head filled with more treasure finds in the attic. He was going on a hunt today.

He met the foundation contractor and escorted him toward the house. He was a big guy, with a belly barely contained by his blue work shirt. It hung over his belt, and his ham-sized hands touched the walls as they descended the external steps into the basement. They went down another set of steps carved from bedrock and entered the subcellar. The walls were made of dirt and stone, the house above them weighing heavily on the support beams. Brad held up a lantern, letting the light pool around them. It was quiet here. Not a sound penetrated the dank interior. He knew the secret room was on the other side of the wall. Their voices were muted in the gloom. Shadows stretched on the whitewashed stone, making them look like distorted giants. Brad stared at walls that seemed to writhe and move as though someone were trapped underneath. He squinted hard, trying to focus in the darkness. Images of handprints feathered across the stone, the fingers gnarled, clutching the surface as though it were a lifeline. It was a play of light, he reasoned. Julie's words from earlier that morning came back to him. Perhaps the energy of past occupants still circulated here. Were the shadowy handprints residual memories or refracting light playing with his vision? A whine like thousands of insects filled his ears, and he shook his head to clear it.

"I hate these old places," the contractor said uneasily. He took out a crumpled handkerchief to wipe the sweat beading on his shiny forehead.

Brad nervously eyed the walls, squinting hard. Everything was hazy, as if the room were filled with smoke. Spots darkened the mossy stone, contracting to dense splashes of gray. They shifted, their patterns ebbing, as though they were breathing. From underneath lowered lashes, he glanced at the other man, wondering if he saw the changing patterns of light as well, but he felt too silly to ask him if he did. A sound like a low moan rent the turgid air. Brad locked his gaze with the contractor, who shrugged, his face devoid of color.

"Did you hear that?" Brad whispered, holding up the lantern so the light reflected off the walls. They slithered, the shadows making them appear as though they were moving. He walked over to touch the cold surface. It was as solid as rock. What else could it be? "For a minute, it looked like someone was there," he laughed. The other man joined him, their mirth changing the entire atmosphere.

"It's the light playing tricks with the stone. Happens all the time. I'm going to have to put in a support beam here." He walked around the dirt floor. "And here." He lifted the bowed wooden boards with competent hands. They heard a loud groan, and their eyes met for an instant. "She's an old lady that needs a facelift—soon."

"How much?"

They haggled a bit, but not much; Brad thought the estimate fair.

"When can you start?" Brad asked.

Though they were alone, Brad had the uneasy feeling that they were in a crowd. The space hummed; in fact, the air vibrated with energy. The area was confined; lazy dust motes floated on the stagnant air. Turning around, he searched the dark corners, looking to see if someone was there. A rat squeaked, causing them both to jump.

The contractor cleared his throat uneasily; his voice was rusty. "I do this all the time, but it never fails—the old places unnerve me." They both laughed. "We will start tomorrow, if that's OK with you?"

"Yeah. Do you want a deposit?"

"I'm not worried about you." They shook and arranged to meet at seven the next morning.

Brad escorted him out, then stood in the rutted driveway for a long time. He looked back at the house, considering it, debating about where to start. He stared at the cellar entrance, wondering if he should go back and examine it again. Pulling a worn baseball cap from his back pocket, he placed it firmly on his head. He walked up the front steps, the boards musically making his presence known.

When Brad got to the double doors, one swung open, inviting him in. It squealed on its hinges, adding to the macabre atmosphere. A laugh bubbled up from his lips. That's all they needed—intruders. *Really*, he thought. *What did they expect to find in this dump?* He cursed, thinking they had had a break-in. He observed the open door. Carefully, he entered, quietly walking through the reception area, his eyes darting around. Looking back, he saw only one set of footprints on the dusty floor. He bent to examine them: there was a single set of tracks and they were his. He stood listening to the silence and knew he was alone. The dust was undisturbed; the house was devoid of all life except for him. Light refracted from the huge chandelier in the main entry, the crystal tinkling gently. Brad looked up to see it swaying, the small ornamental drops clinking against one another. Searching for the source of a breeze, he felt only the decayed, stuffy indoor atmosphere. The chimes danced along his spine to the top of his head, his blood coursing through his veins. Pulsing with energy, he put his hand on the solid banister, placing his foot on the first stair. The upstairs called to him, drawing him toward the attic.

His phone's shrill ring broke the silence, Julie's face lighting the screen. Brad bit his lower lip, unimaginably annoyed by her call. A feeling of impatience welled in his chest, and he found himself fighting the urge to hit ignore. He was in charity with her, wasn't he? he thought. It was good between them, so why did he feel a gargoyle of resentment resting heavily on his shoulder? As if to confirm it, Brad looked over his shoulder, seeing only weak sunlight peeking through the stained glass windows to light the gloom inside.

He swiped his finger and held the phone to his ear. "Hi," he said curtly.

Julie was silent for a moment. "Anything wrong?"

Brad snarled, "Why do you think that, Julie? What is it? I've got things to do."

"Sorry for interrupting your busy day. I just wanted to know what happened with the foundation people."

"I have the proposal. I booked them for tomorrow. It's a quick fix."

Julie sighed. "You hired them?"

"Look, if you want to do this yourself, just say so, and I am out of here." Anger simmered beneath his skin, running like white lightning through his bloodstream. The words, filled with heat, poured out of his mouth, the same one that had kissed her so tenderly that morning and told her that he loved her. It was as if he didn't own his own body.

"Sorry," she snapped. "Usually we discuss the estimates."

"Well, this time we didn't."

"Brad—"

"I don't have time, Julie. I have to get this place cleaned up before Willy gets here to help with the baths and kitchen. I'll see you later." The tension he felt was like a pot boiling over and all his hostility was focused on her. He touched the phone's surface, cutting off her good-bye.

"Tessa, stop tormenting him." Gerald perched himself next to his companion on the railing one flight above Brad.

"Did you see the picture on his phone?" she demanded. "Do you think she is prettier than me?"

"Too thin for my taste." He eyed his preening companion. "I prefer my women a bit more full-figured. You remember, Rubenesque."

"She's as skinny as a drowned cat."

"I wouldn't go that far. Besides, Tessa, my sweet, they like their women like that now. All muscles, like a…like little boys."

"Hah, I knew it! She's flat-chested." She stroked her hands down her well-endowed bosom. "Mine are real. Touch them, Gerald, you'll see."

"With pleasure." He leaned over to caress her, and she flew off the banister to levitate above Brad's head.

"As if," she teased him. "I didn't let you touch them then, and I'm certainly not going to let you now."

Gerald felt his face heat with anger, his hands balling into fists. Tessa and he had come to a sort of comfortable relationship after all these years together. He liked to think of them as an old married couple. Usually it was just the two of them. With the occasional intruder, he allowed Tessa her mild flirtations. And there were the Sentinels, of course. She terrorized the crack addicts—they were so unattractive he had never interfered—but this was a whole different story. Tessa was intrigued. Lit up like an incandescent flame, she was back to her old tricks. She primped in front of her imaginary mirror, singing. He puffed up with indignation. She never did those things for him. He stalked across the landing past the handsome man, filled with resentment.

"He is gorgeous." Tessa taunted Gerald, circling Brad like a predator, her eyes drinking in his muscular build. "Look at his hands; he is so sensitive. I bet he would know how to make me feel like a woman."

"Enough!" Gerald yelled at her, stopping when he saw the satisfied look on her face. Anger never worked with her. They knew each other so well after all these years. She thrived on his pain. Changing his tactics, he teased her instead. "Honey, you're so old, they'd call you a saber-toothed tiger instead of a cougar," Gerald snickered. Tessa's face changed, turning white, her teeth elongating into fangs. She raced back at him, her eyes black pits of coal. "Save it for the tourists, Tessa. Doing that makes you look like an old hag." He floated away, his laughter echoing off the walls.

Brad looked around. He heard something. His gray eyes scanned the high ceilings but could discern nothing in the gloom. He took the stairs lightly, the handrail smooth under his calloused hand. He paused at the Joan of Arc stained glass window, shaking his head. He understood flowers, even animals, but Joan of Arc? There was something eerily depressing about a stained glass window decorated with a martyred saint. He bowed to her gallantly and then bounded up to the next story. Soon he found himself at the top level of the house. A door beckoned to him from the ceiling. There was no rope to pull it down. He looked around, spying an old chair. Climbing up, he reached over his head to pull down the attic door.

The chair wobbled; Brad glanced down the railing, the potential three-story fall giving him vertigo. It was a long way down, he thought, gulping. His bum leg protested, reminding him it was just healed. He reached forward, his fingers scrabbling at the opening. Lurching, he started to weave, feeling himself losing his balance. The air gelled. He thought dispassionately that he was going to fall, and it was going to be messy. Two of the chair's legs lifted off the ratty carpet, and Brad's mouth opened to scream, but no sound came out. Like a manipulated marionette, the chair righted itself, pulling him away from the railing. It landed with a hard thud, jarring him, but he knew he was safe. *That was close*, he thought. He got down shakily and sat on the top stair, his legs wobbly, his heart beating a rapid tattoo in his chest. He wiped the sweat beading his brow. He had almost fallen, of that he was sure. He just didn't know what had prevented it. Taking a deep breath, he climbed onto the chair again, tentatively reaching for the ceiling, latching on to the pull so he could yank open the door to the attic. It fell forward, creaking on its rusty hinges. A blast of hot air hit him full in the face. Heart pounding in his chest, he paused to look back at the chandelier, now that he was at eye level with it. It was a monster, all cut glass in a million small pieces. It appeared to spin slowly, creating a kaleidoscope of rainbow colors. Brad's skin prickled, and he felt the caress of a light breeze travel up his spine.

Tessa drew close to the human. The Sentinel had pulled him to safety. She hated their interference. Just when she had control of a situation, they would step in to block her from doing as she pleased. She was afraid of them and found herself backed into a corner when she felt their presence. The air always thickened, making movement difficult. She glanced around, making sure she was alone. Smiling, she let her hands linger near Brad's face and felt him shudder as she slid them down the back of his body. She longed to press up against him, inhale his maleness, lose herself in his embrace. She swirled through him, lightly caressing his heated skin, willing herself to form, feeling the weight of gravity pull her cells together. The dense sensation of her skin encasing pressed down with crushing weight. Breath crystallized in her lungs; her nose inhaled the deadness of the house and the aliveness of Brad before her. Light hurt her eyes; her fingers blindly reached out to tangle themselves in the long hair cascading down Brad's back. Brad spun, his eyes widening as she took vague shape before his startled face. She was a chimera, the shadow play of light and darkness, indistinct and almost transparent. Pursing her lips, she leaned in to kiss him.

Brad blinked, his eyes wide, when he was distracted by the chandelier to the right of them. It started swirling, faster and faster in a wild dance, spinning in a dazzling array of lights, sparkling in a circular motion, looking like a Catherine wheel. Bright arcs of light were spat from the many branches, hissing as they struck the walls, hitting with the rapidness of a machine gun. Brad ducked, a blast sizzling across his shoulder blades, ripping his shirt and leaving a smoking trail behind it. The pop of the lightbulbs shattered the silence. Brad flew out of Tessa's ghostly embrace to land on the floor, rolling toward the stairs.

"Nooooo. You sent them to torture me, Gerald. I hate you."

Brad heard a female scream as a burst of electricity found him like a heat-seeking missile, creasing the skin above his ear, pushing his head into the wall with a loud *thwack*. Stars exploded inside his head, and he knew nothing more.

Tessa roared with frustration, her semitransparent form shrinking until it disappeared into nothingness. Blackness descended on the landing to surround the unconscious Brad. It hovered over him, obliterating all light and sound. Slowly, two human shapes formed, one bending over the prone man, a long white finger touching his face.

"You were too rough." The voice was in a frequency so high only a dog would hear it.

"He's a big boy." The other being shrugged. It was tall, with a shock of pure white hair. The eyes were a laser blue in its almost transparent face. It wavered, fading in, and grew stronger, becoming more solid.

"Are you going to do anything?" The other form was definitely female, with the same white hair in a neat bun. She was almost as tall as the male. They wore iridescent suits that reflected the weak sunlight. She bent over and caressed Brad's slack face. He groaned, and she rose, hiding her hand behind her thin back.

"We won't have to. He'll remember nothing. We have to go. He can't see us."

"We can't just leave him like this. What if Tessa comes back?"

The male cocked his head. "Gerald is consoling her." He laughed, his bright eyes luminous.

"You frightened her," the female admonished. "You're not supposed to."

"It's what I do best. Come, we must leave. Look, he wakes. He will go to the attic now."

"I think not. He's bruised. You hurt him."

"He has to go into the attic, Marum. Don't interfere."

Marum huffed, walking through the banister to disappear into the woodwork of the opposite wall.

Her companion shook his head and muttered, "Women."

Brad rose on all fours, his nose running, his eyes tearing. He touched the ripped corner of his shirt, feeling the raw skin where the spark had singed him. He looked around, shook his head with disbelief, stood up, and gripped the banister as he weaved just a bit. His phone broke the silence, Julie's face lighting the screen. He pressed ignore and walked toward the stairs to the attic.

CHAPTER EIGHT

J ulie stared glumly at the computer screen, idly looking at pictures of Victorian homes.

"You OK?" Dulcie slid into her seat, a cup of coffee
in one hand, a plate with a doughnut in the other. "Want?"
She held up the plate.

Julie shook her head. "I had my quota of cake yesterday." A faint smile came as the memory of their *Tom Jones*
eating frenzy flashed through her mind. "I feel like I'm
missing something." Julie sighed. She pressed Brad's number again and got his voice mail. "No. Nothing. I think
Brad is mad at me."

"Why?"

"He's so testy. Every time I call him, he has no patience
for me. He's not even answering my call now."

Dulcie ripped apart the doughnut, considering it.
"Stop running after him. The more you push, the more
he'll pull. Don't call him fifty times a day."

"I don't call him that much." Julie stood, outraged.

"Oh yes, you do, and more. I don't call Carlos but
once a day, girl. You got to make them miss you." She

looked at Julie, her dark eyes dancing. "You got to play hard to get. You too easy."

Julie shrugged. "I hate playing games."

Dulcie smiled, revealing even white teeth. "Isn't he playing games by not answering you?"

"Huh!" Julie huffed, considering what Dulcie had said.

Her intercom buzzed with the annoying tenacity of a droning bee, interrupting their conversation. She depressed the button to hear orders rapped out in rapid succession. Go to human resources, get the Bailse contracts, stop by supplies, get a new stapler. Julie took a pen, recording the list so she wouldn't forget anything. With a sigh, she rose, looking at Dulcie for sympathy.

"Better you than me is all I have to say. I got him breakfast, and they put the eggs on the wrong side of his plate." She laughed. "I got him a new plate, but it had more than eggs on it when I gave it to him."

"Eeeew. That's disgusting, Dulce."

"He deserves it. You can't treat people like scum and not pay for it." She harrumphed and turned, her nose in the air, to type the requisition order she had been working on.

Julie giggled and headed off, taking the elevator to her first stop. In the supply room, she found a box to hold all the things Mr. Wilson had demanded. She juggled a heavy stapler, a box of staples, a ruler, pens, and a cord for the new phone. She became aware that someone was in the room but, not feeling threatened, didn't look up to identify the intruder. A hand caressed her bottom and she gasped, pushing away. Strong arms grabbed her from the front, one pushing its way down her blouse.

"Julie." She felt his hot breath heat the back of her neck.

"Mr. Wilson!" She wriggled away from him. He was a short man with a wide belly. Surely, he couldn't be doing this to her. "Stop! What are you doing?" His pasty bald head gleamed with sweat.

"Julie, Julie, Julie." He pressed his groin against her. She felt him poking her, and she used her elbow to break his embrace. "Don't you feel the tension between us? Dump that pretty boy. We could do great things together." His glasses were askew on his face, his lips wet with drool, his eyelids at half-mast in what she guessed was his bedroom look.

A giggle bubbled up hysterically from her throat. "Stop that this instant!" she shouted, as his hands groped to separate her white shirt from her skirt.

"I know you want it. Just think of what I can give you. Julie, I can make life very easy for you."

"I'm married," she said sternly, slapping his hand away. The box of supplies was crushed between them, some of its contents falling out the sides.

"I…want…you…now!" he spat. "I always get what I want." His hot eyes devoured her.

Julie looked at his pursed lips and his unfocused gaze and yelled, "I am not interested! I said stop it!" When he didn't respond, she reached for the ruler between them and slapped him on his fleshy cheek, drawing blood.

Mr. Wilson gasped, his pudgy hand going to his cheek. His face crumpled.

"Oh!" She dropped the ruler. She hadn't meant to hurt him, but she wouldn't let him take advantage of her. "Oh!"

"I thought you wanted it." Her boss backed away. "You always wear such short skirts. You bend in front of me."

"You keep dropping things," Julie defended herself. "Mr. Wilson, I don't think I can be here anymore."

"Neither do I. Are you going to lodge a complaint? Because if you do, I will say that you asked for it."

"Asked for it! I don't know what you are talking about. You're despicable, Mr. Wilson. I thought of you as a father figure."

"Me?" he asked with a laugh. "A father figure? I could have any girl I want." He stalked to the door. "You make trouble, and I will make sure you never see another construction loan from the bank again."

Julie put the supplies on a shelf, walked to her desk, and emptied the drawers.

"Where you going?" Dulcie looked up from her screen.

"I got a better offer. See you, Dulcie. I'm leaving, and I won't be back."

CHAPTER NINE

Brad climbed the steep stairs into the overheated attic. He felt the bruise over his ear. It was tender to the touch, but nothing worse. He had blacked out for a minute. Well, Julie had warned him not to go into the attic alone. The last time, he had fallen ten feet and broken his leg in two places. It was a bitch of an injury. Four years in the heat and danger of Afghanistan without a scratch, but in one of his first flips, he almost incapacitated himself. No Purple Heart in flipping houses. He rubbed the permanent bump in his shin, wincing at its tenderness. Maybe he should listen to her, maybe not. It was stifling up there, with the acrid smell of dry wood and insects. Using his phone as a flashlight, he lit a path, his mouth open with wonder. It was a treasure trove of furniture, bronzes, boxes of dishes, Majolica ware, Wedgwood china, and rows and rows of belongings from different eras. Brad smiled; this could be life changing.

He wove between the aisles, opening a box here, moving a painting there, knowing it was going to take weeks to go through and catalog all the material. Pulling up an old cracked leather campaign chair that probably dated from the War of 1812, he randomly picked a box and started to go through it. He pulled out a yellow satin gown, wrapped in crisp paper, the folds releasing a faint scent of roses. Something dropped; Brad bent over to pick it up. It was a delicate fan made from bamboo and chicken skin, with a painted scene of graceful Asian ladies covering its surface.

"Oh, Gerald," Tessa sighed. "It's my fan. I thought I'd never see it again. I almost threw it away, and then, when…you know." She paused, her big eyes watching him. She waltzed elegantly around the room, humming, her face dreamy. She stopped to look at her companion and told him, "When you disappeared, I decided to keep it. I packed it away and then couldn't find it. I thought it was lost. He's found it."

"It was never lost," Gerald replied softly.

CHAPTER TEN

1862

"La, Gerry, get me some more punch. I swear I am parched." Tessa directed a tall blond man in the crowd surrounding her to fetch the refreshment.

Gerald rolled his eyes, hating to leave her with four other admirers, but he still went to get her a drink.

The room was filled with soldiers, their blue uniforms with shiny brass buttons reflecting the warm glow from the gas chandeliers. He nodded to his cousin, a Union captain, who was caught up in a conversation with Tessa's father. He was a railroad man, Frank Hemmings. Rich as Croesus, smart as a fox, at the turn of the century he had started a ferry business from Long Island to Connecticut, making a fortune that had led to an even bigger one when his trains opened up the West. Gerald knew all the details, as his family financed most of Hemmings's business ventures. He had recently left his safe bank position to join up. It had caused a huge fight. Only the agreement that he would work in Washington on the general's staff quieted his father's opposition. He hoped that Tessa would notice him now that he was dressed in blue. Though only a lowly lieutenant, he had the important job of being adjunct to General McClellan. It was an easy appointment that his neighbor, Frank Hemmings, had been able to secure for him. The general had worked with Hemmings at the Illinois Central Railroad. When Lincoln appointed him general-in-chief of all the Union armies, Gerald volunteered and was given a position in Washington to help move supplies to the troops. Though he was horse mad, he was in no hurry to get himself killed. Let Lewis run around playing soldier on the front lines. He was content doing his share in Washington, coming home for brief visits and keeping his eye on Tessa. She didn't know she was going to be his wife. Let her enjoy her flirtations, the attention of all her admirers. As long as they ended up together, he didn't much care about the rest.

Nothing but the best for Frank Hemmings. A string quartet played in the corner of the vast parlor. Silver dishes and trays held steaming food. The punch bowl, a family heirloom made by Paul Revere himself, rested in the center of the giant buffet, fruit floating on the surface of the iced punch.

"She is beautiful." Lewis came up next to him, watching their hostess. He had a black handlebar mustache, lean cheeks, and fierce eyes. He raised his silver cup to salute her with an appreciative grin.

"Hands off, cousin. Mine," Gerald snarled.

Lewis was both older and taller, with an air of sophistication that always turned a lady's head. Long hair skimmed his collar; he stood at ease, a faint smile on his thin lips.

"You haven't declared yourself yet, Gerry. As far as I'm concerned, it's open season."

Gerald pulled a eight-inch object from his pocket. He opened it, making sure the fan was still as perfect as when he had purchased it. "Don't poach on my preserve, Lewis. I believe I've made my intentions clear."

"To everyone but the lady, it seems." Lewis laughed, as he gestured toward the retreating back of Tessa, who was leaving the room to walk in the gardens with another man. "Hunting season has just started." Pulling a flask from his breast pocket, Lewis offered his cousin a sip. Gerald declined, leaving both Lewis and the punch at the buffet.

Gerald bit the end of a Spanish cigar as he leaned against the frame of the French doors leading out to the garden. Jasmine perfumed the air; strains of the violins seeped out into the night air. It was chilly, and he wondered if Tessa had her wrap. He sucked hard on his cigar, the glowing tip the only evidence of his presence. He heard a giggle followed by a smothered gasp. She was being kissed. He felt his face redden with embarrassment. She was supposed to be his; they had an informal agreement. He ground his cigar purposefully into a planter, leaving only a taste of bitterness in his mouth. His cousin's smile mocked him from across the room. Gerald's collar felt too tight. He ran a finger around the inside, knowing everybody was watching him with a mixture of curiosity and pity. What was she thinking? They were promised to each other, yet she took every opportunity to tease and flirt with other men. He joined the army for her to notice him, and his uniform brought nothing but contemptuous remarks from her. He was only a lieutenant; he wouldn't see action; how was she supposed to brag to the other ladies?

Tessa's companion, her mousy governess, peered through the darkness, looking for her charge. "She's over there." He pointed to the rustling bushes. "You'd better get her out of there before you have to explain where she's been to her father." He spun on his polished heel and stalked away from the spot.

Tessa's mother introduced Gerald to Lady Pamela Winters, the duke of Eversham's daughter. Tessa had inherited her mother's good looks as well as her titian hair. Mrs. Hemmings was busty but not as tall as her daughter. She trilled when she put Lady Pamela's gloved hand in Gerald's and pushed them onto the dance floor. The duke's daughter was visiting—quite a coup for the Hemmings family—and in need of a husband. Preferably a wealthy one to trade an old titled family name in exchange for a cash infusion. Gerald listened to her inane chatter as they glided on the polished parquet floor, his eyes never leaving the French doors.

Tessa slipped in, her hair mussed, her fingers adjusting her dress. Their eyes met; a brittle smile graced her lips, her eyes were bright in her flushed face. Gerald sighed deeply. She was so beautiful. She was a jade, a flirt, but he just couldn't get himself to care. It bothered both his parents, but Gerald knew his own mind, and the only woman on it was Tessa. He had known her for years; their families celebrated yearly events together as the premier social scions of the area. It seemed she always turned to him, using him for excuses to her parents when she broke the rules. Gerald sensed when she would need his protection and somehow always managed to be at the right place to bail her out. She was as mischievous as a kitten, as daring as a lion, and the only person in the world who touched his heart. He loved her to distraction, and though he knew she used him shamelessly, it didn't diminish the fierceness he felt for her.

He handed Lady Pamela off to Kurt Hemmings, Tessa's older brother and perhaps the lady's future. Kurt bowed over her hand, his long auburn hair curling charmingly around his pale face. He was a poet, with brooding eyes coupled with a practiced air of ennui that drove females mad. Gerald looked at Lady Pamela's faintly bovine face, noticing the vacant look, and wondered when she'd start to drool over the son of the house. A match made in heaven, they would have poetic, chesty, mildly bored children with cow-like eyes and placid personalities. He wondered what kind of offspring he would have with Tessa—if only she would hold still long enough for him to make her realize that he would make her happy.

A firm slap on his back returned him to the present. Frank Hemmings squeezed his shoulder. He was mildly drunk, his bloodshot eyes watching his son with distaste.

"How is the general treating you, m'boy?" he inquired.

Gerald turned to see the naked disdain on Hemmings's face as he watched his son take out a handkerchief and wave it around as he recited one of his many poems.

"Little Napoleon?" Gerald smiled, calling the general by his nickname. "He's an interesting man."

"Do you call him that to his face? Didn't think so. Graduated top of his class. Organized the Illinois for me."

"He is a great leader. The men like him."

"When do you return?"

"Monday next. I report to Washington."

"Proud of you, son. Right proud. You could have taken the easy way out, like some," he sneered. "Chose to represent your house like a man." He harrumphed. "What do you make of my boy?"

"He's young yet, Frank."

They stood in silence. Hemmings watched his son. Gerald stared at Tessa.

"Step into the library with me. I have some brandy and a cigar I've been saving for you. Not that schizer you like to smoke." He motioned to the cigars resting under Gerald's jacket.

Tessa danced past them in the arms of yet another man, her face lit with joy. Their eyes met for an instant, and then she looked away. He couldn't even hold her gaze for a long period of time. Both men observed her spinning past them to end one dance and begin another in a new set of arms.

"Gerald," Hemmings said abruptly, "I want a word with you."

Gerald followed the older man into the library, taking a seat in one of the deep leather chairs. Frank Hemmings closed the door, poured a brandy, and handed it to Gerald.

"What's this I hear about Lincoln and McClellan?" he asked baldly, never a man to beat around the bush.

Gerald sipped the liquor, letting the burn ease his aching heart. "What do you mean, sir?"

"Don't play stupid with me, boy. If I hadn't written the letter, you'd be with Burnside in New Orleans. What in holy hell is going on?"

"You know the general."

Hemmings inclined his head.

Gerald continued, "He is an amazing organizer. He's whipped the Army of the Potomac into a fighting machine. We'll crush the rebs in no time."

"So what's the problem?"

"He's antagonized Lincoln and his staff. I fear the president means to remove him."

Hemmings set down his drink.

Gerald went on, "It's those Pinkerton agents he's surrounded himself with. Their reports make him doubt the strength of the Union army. He's hesitating, and it's making Congress angry."

"Lincoln's losing patience," Hemmings stated. "It will be a mistake if he replaces him."

Gerald agreed. "He's organized the entire army. The men revere him. Yes, it will be a big mistake."

"Can you say something?"

"Frank," Gerald laughed, "I am nothing more than a cog in the wheel there. While at home, I can run a bank; there, I am a lowly lieutenant."

"For now," Frank agreed. "Listen, Gerald, if things go bad, I have to know my little girl is protected."

Gerald put his hand over his chest. "I love Tessa with my whole heart. She will always be safe."

"I can't depend on Kurt. His head is in the clouds."

"No need to worry, Frank. Long Island is a long way from the South."

"Lee is aggressive. He won't stop at Washington."

"He won't have the chance to get past Washington," Gerald told him confidently. "Lincoln will not allow the capitol to be burned again."

"I wish I could be as sure as you. I leave for London in a week. Kurt is staying here to entertain the duke's daughter. You will watch out for Tessa." It was a statement.

"I will be back and forth over the next two months. I have to visit factories making the guns in Connecticut. I will make sure to stop by each time I return north. Surely you realize, Frank, that I will always watch over Tessa."

They shook hands; it would be the last time they ever saw each other.

The party was winding down, the spring air cooling the heated room. Many had left. Kurt Hemmings sat in a corner in rapt conversation with Lady Pamela, her bulbous eyes concentrating on his full lips.

Tessa stood beside the fireplace, her tired eyes staring into the flames.

"Are you too tired for a dance?" he asked softly.

Tessa spun to see Gerald standing behind her.

"I'm never too tired for a dance." Her dark eyes darted behind him, looking for someone else.

"You've danced with everyone at least twice. There is no one left but me, Tessa," he snapped.

"There is always someone else." She watched her words cut him. He was easy to hurt, wore his devotion for everyone to see. It wasn't her fault. She considered his bland blond hair and droopy brown eyes. He was just so damn boring. She sighed.

"Not tonight." He grabbed her waist, pulling her possessively to him.

Tessa inclined her head sideways, looking at him calmly. "There's always going to be another man, Gerald, no matter how tightly you hold me," she whispered, a faint smile on her lips.

They waltzed around the room silently, Gerald's lips a grim white line, Tessa's face serene, her eyes dreamy. He caught himself looking at her, the rose hue of her skin, her sable lashes touching her plump cheeks, her dewy pout.

Tessa lifted her face to look at his mouth and then they locked eyes. No words passed between them, but she licked her lips, feeling his hold tighten. One side of her mouth lifted, and she said only for his ears, "It won't matter how tightly you hold me, Gerry. I can't help who I am."

Gerald spun her around the room, closer to the music, where he couldn't hear the words hitting him with the same pain as bullets.

The last dance ended with a smattering of applause, mixed with tired sighs. She curtsied daintily, saying, "Always a pleasure, Gerry."

Gerald bowed stiffly. "I don't know why I love you, Tessa, but God help me, I do." He pulled the fan from inside his uniform. "I brought this back for you from Washington. Hopefully it will cool your ardor."

"A fan. How nice." She opened the fan, using it to flirt with him. She would flirt with the dustman if she could, and they both knew it. "Are you are leaving me this token as a reminder of you?"

"I don't want you to forget me."

"Do you think you're forgettable?" she taunted, her eyes sparkling. "I never forget anybody."

Their eyes met over the chicken-skin fan, and Gerald sighed, thinking of the many available men that would be left to dance with her after he returned to the war.

He escorted her back to a crowd of young women giggling in the corner. He bowed elegantly, and Tessa watched his retreating back as he left, a grim look on his face. She didn't know why she couldn't love him. He was amiable enough, richer than her father, respected in the community. His blond hair was parted neatly, his skin clear, his figure trim from all the riding. Yet no matter how much she knew he loved her, Tessa couldn't keep her eyes from watching every other man in the room. There was Howard with his bright blue eyes, and Thaddeus with his wicked smile, and Lewis, who knew how to make a woman feel all tingly. How could her father expect her to settle on just one man, when there were so many? As soon as one walked away, there were ten more with hungry smiles on their lips, admiration in their faces. Tessa felt her insides bubble with anticipation. Men and their compliments made her skin glow, her lips swell, and her heart beat faster. How could she think that Gerald was all she needed? she wondered. Tessa looked at the fan, considering the Asian ladies painted on it. Their feet had been bound, so they were unnaturally tiny. It was a mark of aristocracy—or, she frowned, imprisonment. With their crippled feet, their freedom was curtailed. Hobbled and riddled with pain, all they could do was sit and be available. Trapped with a single man whether they liked him or not. She dropped the fan onto a passing tray with dirty glasses. Gerald caught her look of distaste as she discarded his gift. The music began, and Tessa found herself pulled into yet another set of strong arms, the embrace on the verge of too tight, the breath of desire filling her lungs.

The party wore on into the night. The room had closed in on Gerald. Too much heavy perfume, too much smoke from the gas lamps. Too much Tessa, teasing him with other men. His eyes smarted; his throat burned. He wandered out into the gardens, the cooler air having forced lovers back into the heated corners of the main salon. He lit a cheroot, inhaling deeply, letting the bite of the tobacco take away his bitterness.

Gerald leaned against the iron gates, the early morning dew turning the grass silver. Horses neighed, and the distant sound of men carousing on Bedlam Street by the harbor carried across the chill night. He debated walking down to the tavern to spend the remainder of his night there, when a rustling deep in the bushes disturbed the peace of the early morning hours. Grinding out his cigar, he turned, listening to feet scrambling through the foliage. Quietly, Gerald edged up the long drive to stand in a thicket behind a huge maple tree, its trunk as broad as a man's back. Whispered words carried in the sharp air, gravel crunching with urgency. A man in evening dress walked quickly from the trees, four people trailing behind him. Lighting the way with a single lantern, Kurt Hemmings led four escaping slaves—crouched low, dressed in rags— toward the basement entrance of the house.

A twig snapped and everyone froze. Gerald could hear the harsh breathing of the four escapees. Kurt lifted a revolver in his direction, his face no longer soft and dreamy but hard with determination mixed with fear.

"It's me, Kurt." Gerald appeared, his hands raised.

"What are you doing here?" Kurt demanded, the poet's voice gone.

"I was blowing a cloud. What's going on?" He looked at the four runaways behind Kurt.

"What do you think?"

"You're a guide?"

"No, a station master," he said, referring to those who participated in the Underground Railroad. They set up safe houses where escaping slaves could stay on their journey to freedom in Canada. It was illegal as well as dangerous. Gerald could see there were three men and a female. They were frightened, standing close to Kurt as though he were a human shield. One was injured; his left thigh had a filthy cloth covering a bleeding wound. One of the bigger men was holding him up. "Follow me," Kurt whispered urgently. "I have to tuck them away, and then we'll talk."

"You're hiding fugitives? You're in the Underground Railroad?" Gerald whispered furiously as they walked in a group to the house's basement entrance. Kurt urged him to be quiet.

Gerald followed them through the entrance, where Kurt used a key on a rusty lock. He opened the door, urging them in. Gerald heard their bare feet padding down the stone steps into a cellar beneath the basement. Though he had played here with both Kurt and Tessa, he never knew of the existence of the room he soon found himself in. The lantern lit the inky darkness, and Kurt whispered, "Almost there." Kurt's long fingers felt along the wall until he depressed a spot and a small door swung open. Bending over, the woman rushed in, followed by the rest.

"You have to keep your voices low." Kurt got on his knees to distribute supplies. He rolled out an army bedroll. "There are bandages, water, and food. I will be back tomorrow and direct you to the next station."

They lowered the groaning man to the bed.

"This man needs a doctor." Gerald bent down to examine his leg.

"Impossible," Kurt responded. He turned to the woman. "You are so close, so close to heaven."

"Praise God." The woman fell to her knees, tears streaming down her face.

"You followed the signs?"

"Left foot, peg foot," one of the men offered. It was one of the trails they used to guide slaves to different safe houses. He was broad-shouldered and tall, with huge calloused hands.

The smaller man bent down to tend to the wound on his friend's leg. Gerald saw that the wounded one was little more than a child, perhaps twelve or thirteen, no more. He got on one knee and lifted the ragged edge of his pants. The boy skittered away, and Gerald grabbed his leg. "Stop. I won't hurt you." The wound was festering and swollen, with red streaks traveling up his leg. It was hot to the touch. "Kurt, he won't make it."

"The slave catcher almost got us. He shot Cicero," the big slave told them.

The woman took a cloth to wash the wound.

Kurt hunkered down, putting the lantern on the floor. "Where?"

"Two days south of here. We hid—"

"I know where you hid," Kurt interrupted him. "We may have to keep you a day longer." He touched the young man's burning forehead. "You won't mind our Northern hospitality, I'm thinking." He rose, motioning for Gerald to join him. "Do what you can for him," he told the fugitives. "I'll see what else I can arrange. Remember to keep quiet." He left them the lantern and closed the door to their hideout.

"Are you crazy?" Gerald rounded on him as soon as they left the basement.

"Are you?" Kurt responded coolly.

"This is madness," Gerald insisted.

"Yes. It is," Kurt said quietly. He caught Gerald's arm. "You won't tell?"

Gerald looked him full in the face. "You put your whole family at risk. Does your father know?"

They locked eyes, the silence heavy between them.

Kurt shook his head. "Does it matter? To me, this is more effective than being cannon fodder. I can really make a difference doing this."

"That boy needs a doctor."

"I can't risk it. If they are found out, local judges are paid to rule against letting them go."

"What?" Gerald asked incredulously.

"They get ten dollars a head to cooperate and return them to their owners. It's too risky. I don't know if Doc Newton will report them." He paused and exhaled a long sigh. "I don't know what he'll do. There are so many of them."

"How many?"

Kurt shrugged. "I've helped twenty-two escape to heaven."

"Heaven?" Gerald asked.

"Canada," Kurt repeated. "Not all wars are fought on a battleground, Gerald. You do your part; I do mine."

CHAPTER ELEVEN

J ulie didn't realize she was shaking until she tried to reach Brad. Her finger trembled so much, she tapped on his number and ended up calling DirecTV instead. Clutching her phone to her chest, she closed her eyes, forcing herself to calm down. Taking long, slow breaths, she replayed Mr. Wilson's attack, outrage filling her chest. Her cheeks burned, righteous anger replacing the fear. Calmer now, she looked at her phone. Thoughts tumbled through her head. She could start a lawsuit, but the banker she worked with was Mr. Wilson's best friend. Her boss had introduced them and cosigned the first loan they had taken out. He had done it as a favor, when every bank had amped up requirements after the whole mortgage meltdown. Financing was so tough. They had barely made a dent in their home mortgage and had next to nothing in equity. He had done them an enormous favor. It was a small bank, and Mr. Wilson was their largest customer. What would she do if they called in her construction loan? How was Brad going to react? Her finger paused over his name. What if he went after Mr. Wilson? Brad was a big guy, and she knew, when provoked, he could get angry enough to administer some rough justice. What if he punched him? Brad could go to jail. Tears sprang to her eyes. They would have to dump the house as fast as possible and hope the bank would continue working with them. *Oh, we are screwed,* Julie thought, panic replacing her heat. *My boss screwed me. Without touching me, he managed to really screw me.*

By the time she got home, her heart was heavy. She'd had that job for nine years, and there was never a hint of anything from her boss. She couldn't go back, that was for certain. Her mind feverishly went over her limited options. She had quit, so unemployment was out of the question. She threw her keys onto the pitted Formica countertop and quickly stripped off her clothes. Turning on the hot water in the shower, she let it steam up the bathroom, hoping it would clean the dirty feeling away. Julie stopped in her tracks, wrapping an oversized white towel around herself. Spinning slowly, she felt violated, as if she were being observed.

"Brad?" she called softly. Opening the door to one of the extra bedrooms, she looked around, taking in its sparseness. She walked into the living room, noting her husband had taken both the paintings and the box. He must have brought them to Sal's, she reasoned, as a chill shook her body. *Delayed shock*, she thought, her eyes darting around the room. Shaking her head, Julie raced to the bathroom, closing the door firmly as if to lock herself away from the world.

Tessa emerged from Brad's closet, where she had been caressing his clothing. His manly scent permeated the enclosed space. She oozed into his shirts, squeezed into his pants, played with his shoes. He was a male, every inch of him. She skittered around the house, flipping through their wedding album, hissing angrily at the picture of Julie wrapped in his arms, bathed by the sunset. Her white dress billowed in the breeze; they were both barefoot and happy, absorbed in each other, the sun lighting their faces.

Tessa trolled through Julie's drawers, slithering among the frilly lace thongs, wondering what they could possibly do for the figure. She smiled, materializing, running her hands down her voluptuous body. *What figure?* she thought. The girl was as flat as a board.

She tried the bathroom door, letting the knob spin in her vaporous hands. Julie was washing her hair, a giant bubbly pile of suds topping it, her eyes closed. Tessa surrounded her.

Julie's eyes sprang open. Instinctively, she covered her private parts, shampoo running from her forehead to sting her eyes. "Ow," she complained, putting her face to the hot water to rinse her eyes. They stung with the burn of a bee sting, and though she wanted to look around, they hurt too much. She placed the towel on her face to dry them, hoping it would stop the sensation.

As soon as she was able, Julie pushed the curtain aside to look at the empty room. Shrugging and feeling foolish, she returned to the shower, rinsing her hair first to get rid of the shampoo once and for all. Silly as she felt, she wanted to finish her shower, wrap herself in Brad's robe, and make a drink.

Tessa left the bathroom to wander into the kitchen. She spied an old outlet over the dilapidated counter that she looked at with distaste. "I'm probably doing you both a favor." She turned transparent, then vaporous, becoming a thin stream of smoke to disappear inside the outlet. Seconds later, the outlet sparked, flames shooting out to catch on the paper towels hanging from their holder. Both the roll of paper towels and the plastic holder lit up, spreading flames across the counter that then jumped onto the floor. Flames danced to the living room, igniting the Berber rug.

Tessa laughed as she rose above the flames, knocking over Julie's purse to watch her exposed license shrivel into ash.

Smoke replaced steam, and the small bathroom filled with it. Julie moved the curtain, turning off the water to stare at the smoke drifting in under the bottom of the door. Sopping wet, she wrapped up in Brad's oversized robe and then grabbed the bathroom doorknob with her slippery hands. The knob sizzled against her skin, and she released it with a curse, panic filling her. She tried using a towel to open the door, but the material would not catch on the knob. It was getting hard to breathe; her body was wracked by coughs. Panting with terror, Julie clutched the doorknob, the pain of the heat nothing compared to the fear filling her heart. It jiggled uselessly. Taking a huge bottle of mouthwash, she pounded at the knob, tears springing to her eyes. She was trapped. The air was thick with smoke; Julie doubled over, having a hard time breathing. With both hands, she turned the knob desperately. The door gave, opening into an inferno. Covering her head with a towel, Julie dashed out the front door, escaping into the fresh air and hearing the sound of sirens wailing in the street.

Later, draped in a blanket, she sat in the back of a police car until an ambulance came, watching despairingly as her little house burned to the ground.

Brad met her at the hospital, his face white with worry.

"What happened?" He brushed her smoky hair from her face.

She sat cross-legged on the bed, wearing a pair of blue hospital scrubs under his robe. She looked fragile and small, dark circles under her eyes. A tight line parted her brows. He touched it gently with his finger, trying to erase it. His usually loquacious wife was strangely subdued. Julie's lower lip trembled, a sob welling in her throat. Her green eyes were huge in her pale face. She opened her mouth to speak, but no sound came out. She reached for him, allowing him to encase her in his arms. He hugged her close, and Julie felt safe again.

"Did you leave the stove on?" he asked after he kissed her head.

Julie shook her head. "Why do you think it's always me?" she whined, her throat raw from the smoke.

The nurse came over with discharge papers. "She's got burned hands. Here's a scrip for the antibiotic cream. Keep them dry." She handed the stack to Brad. "The doctor gave her a mild sedative. She was pretty hysterical when she came in. She can wear the scrubs I gave her home. She came in with just a bathrobe."

A wheelchair was rolled over, and Julie slid off the bed to hobble over to it.

"What happened to your foot?"

"She twisted her ankle when she ran out of the house. Keep the foot elevated," the nurse told him.

Brad wheeled her to his truck, picked her up, and placed her in the cab. "Can you fasten your seat belt? Did they feed you?"

Julie clumsily buckled the belt, sighed, and leaned her head back on the leather seat.

"Jules," Brad asked as he slid into the truck, "did you eat?"

"No. Not hungry."

Brad started the engine. "I think you'll feel better after we get something in your stomach."

"Brad." She looked at him with horror. "Where are we going to go? The house is gone."

"After we eat, I'll go to Bed Bath & Beyond. I'll pick up a few things, and we'll sleep in Bedlam House."

"It's a wreck."

"We can bed down in the main salon. The master bath isn't that bad. We'll make do, Julie. Clothes are going to be a problem. You're probably going to have to call in sick tomorrow as it is."

"Work," she whispered. "Jeez. I have to talk to you about work. I'm too tired. I'm really tired."

"Relax, babe." He took her hand and kissed her knuckles. "We have all the time in the world. We'll talk tonight."

Brad picked up burgers. Julie ate hers in the car while he did a quick shop at the home store. In record time, he had an air mattress, bedding, a microwave, a few pots, and utensils. He felt like he was setting up a dorm room. By the time he got back, Julie was dozing, her head wedged between the window and the seat belt. He made a quick stop at CVS, buying toothbrushes, soap, shampoo, things he thought they'd need. Tomorrow, he'd pick up a few changes of clothes at a department store. He ate while he drove, the meat stone cold, the fries a soggy mess. Julie had picked at hers, eating less than half. Bedlam House was pitch-dark when they arrived. He unloaded the mattress, threw a new sheet on it, then went back to carry his wife into the house. She barely moved. He set her down fully dressed, covering her tenderly with the quilt. Julie coughed, reaching for him. Brad patted her back, then kissed her, lingering over her face, inhaling the residual smell of the smoke. He brushed her hair from her pale cheek, smiling when she sighed and mumbled some nonsensical phrase.

He left a shuttered camping lantern on the floor nearby, pointing its light to the opposite wall so it chased the utter darkness from the room. Satisfied that Julie was deeply asleep, he carted in the rest of their supplies, putting them in neat piles so he could sort them out the next day. He ran barefoot outside to a woodpile, grabbed a few larger pieces plus dry kindling, and ran back in, his feet freezing on the cold October grass. He waited for all his balled-up newspapers to catch, and built up a nice fire in the large fireplace, the hiss and crackle of the wood comforting. He then placed a heavy wrought-iron fire screen in front of the blaze. It warmed the room; the flames painted the walls a comforting buttery color. The side of his face heated, the smell of the burning wood reminding him of home. He glanced at Julie and at the fire, feeling nostalgic. The apple wood smell reminded him of his own boyhood. This was a big house, something his own family had dreamed of their whole lives. The fire danced on the stained glass windows, lighting Joan of Arc's face, chasing the homey feeling away. Brad chucked off his clothes, sliding into the cold sheets to pull the warm body of his wife next to him. They were cheap sheets, not the Egyptian cotton ones Julie liked to buy. They smelled new. They had a chemical odor and irritated his skin. He wrapped himself around his wife, inhaling her scent, closing his eyes with contentment. She purred, stroking his naked chest, and he stilled her bandaged hands with a smile. Julie fit perfectly under his head. Gathering her close, he kissed her, enclosing them both securely in the cocoon of the blankets.

Tessa watched in rapt silence as Brad took care of his wife.

"They are a pretty couple," Gerald observed.

"She's a mouse. She's not woman enough for him." Tessa dripped with jealousy.

"And you are speaking from your vast store of knowledge of him?" Gerald lit a cigar.

"I hate those things." She attempted to grab it, but Gerald ducked out of the way.

"Leave them alone, Tessa. You are only going to anger the Sentinels."

"They are a myth!" she shouted back.

"Oh, you think so, my own?"

"I am not your own!" Tessa spat. "Go away. Leave. I didn't want you then, and I don't want you now! Why don't you just scurry away if you don't want to watch?" Her voice was filled with venom.

Anger turned Gerald red. He started to respond and wondered indeed what he was still doing here. Bristling with frustration, he dissipated into a cloud to dissolve into the night.

Tessa eased under the covers, sliding up against the two bodies, settling on the warm flesh of the woman, to fade into her skin.

Something woke Brad. His wife was writhing against him, her hands clutching, pinching his skin. Julie grabbed his face, her bandaged hands holding him immobile, her mouth opening aggressively over his. She rolled on top of him, her legs sliding around him like tentacles.

"Jules," he whispered.

She bit his lower lip. He kissed her back, holding her tightly. Her mewing sounds became growls. She ripped at her clothes, her eyes closed, the darkness hiding her face. She sat up, pulling the scrubs from the hospital over her head. Her small breasts looked like polished marble in the night. She slid out of the pants, wordlessly mounting Brad. Bending over, she locked her face to his, kissing him rapidly, panting.

"Are you up for this?" he asked between her desperate kisses.

Julie didn't answer with words. She slid down the length of him, shocking him with her heat and aggression. She was insatiable, rocking against him violently. Brad grabbed her, trying to slow her down. He cupped her face, pulling her to him for a soul-searing kiss. Her eyes opened, glowing red, and Brad's breath caught in his throat. Grabbing her shoulders, he forced her flat. Her hair caught in his fingers and he heard her hiss as the strands parted from her skull. "Sorry. Slow down," he urged. She fought with him, sloppily hitting his imprisoning hands. She suddenly stilled, her hands falling uselessly to her sides.

"Jules," he whispered. She was out of it. He heard her shudder, her breathing becoming so deep that Brad rested his head on her chest to hear the slow thud of her heart. Scrambling out of the bed, he forced his own breathing to calm. She wasn't herself. It had to be the drugs they had given her. He looked back at her frowning face. She rolled into a ball, her hands under her cheek, looking young and innocent. Brad stood, shaking his head. Walking to the camping lantern, he crouched down to dim the light. A few long hairs were tangled in his fingers. Putting them up to the light, he sat down heavily. They were reddish-gold.

Brad dressed, too troubled to sleep. He rolled the hairs into a small knot, fitting them in the pocket of his tight jeans. He wasn't going to be able to close his eyes. There had to be an explanation for the red hair. Maybe she had put in extensions and he hadn't noticed. Throbbing with unspent energy, he decided to use it toward cleaning one of the many bathrooms. It was silent in the house; his brain was in overdrive. He loved this part of the night. It was quiet, and it allowed him to lose himself in any job he chose to do. He could work for hours uninterrupted.

Taking another lantern, he went into the primitive bath-room at the top of the stairs to scrub away the grime of neglect from the white tiles. Dawn poked through the filthy windows, painting boxes of sunlight on the floor. Brad emerged from the bathroom newly showered, his hair curling damply around his face. He had set up a homey spot for each of them on the sink with mouth-wash, toothpaste, toothbrushes, a hairbrush—all the things that said normal—but all he was hearing were the screams in his head that something was not.

Barefoot, he tripped down the curved staircase and checked on Julie, who was still in the same position as last night. He saw a big brown van pull up, and a smile broke over his face. The cavalry had arrived.

Willy Watson, six-foot-three, a mighty wall of muscle with a head full of long dreadlocks, bounded up the long gravel drive holding a bag from McDonald's and a card-board tray with two cups of coffee. He tossed away his cigarette before climbing up the porch steps. Julie didn't hold with smoking in her flips. He loved Brad like a brother, even though they had nothing in common except serving together in Afghanistan. His mother's family came from the Deep South, but he'd been brought up with his father's family in Harlem, enlisting rather than joining a gang on the streets. The only Maine he'd ever heard of was Main Street in Flushing, until he met Brad and heard about his folksy, country background. He was a good man who recognized another good man. While they served, Brad lost both his parents, and Willy urged him to relo-cate to New York. Then he met Julie, his firecracker of a wife, and they formed an informal partnership. Brad and Julie were his ticket out of Harlem. One more flip, and he'd have enough to buy a small house in St. Albans and marry Rita, his baby's mama. He had negotiated with Sal for a small ring from the antique shop. With the proceeds from this house, Willy would be able to pay off the balance. He had gone down to Charlotte to break the news to his own mama. There was going to be a wedding this summer.

Brad opened the door before he had a chance to knock. He held his finger over his mouth, indicating that Willy should be quiet.

Willy held up the greasy bag, saying, "Mickey Dee's."

Brad nodded with a smile, slipped on his hoodie, bummed a cigarette, and sat down heavily on the porch.

"I didn't expect you to be here yet," Willy said as he sat down next to him.

"Me neither."

Willy unwrapped an Egg McMuffin. "You want this one or the sausage?"

Brad shrugged. "I don't care. I'll take anything. You were supposed to be back Monday." Brad accepted the breakfast sandwich and placed the coffee on the other side of him.

"Took care of business." He shrugged. "I missed Rita and LaMarr too much."

Brad nodded. "Yeah. A lot's been going on. Our house burned down."

"No shit!" The expletive rolled off Willy's tongue. "Patricia Lane? Completely?"

"Like it was bombed."

"Julie OK?"

"She burned her hands."

"What? She was in the house?"

"Yep. She barely made it out."

"Sheeeet. She at her sister's?"

"Nah." Brad shook his head. "She's sleeping inside. Some crazy shit, man."

"What you gonna do?"

"We're camping out here for now. It's as good a place as any. I have to get working on the insurance claim. Once we get the replacement money, we can look for a place to rent." Brad looked in the bag. "How many of these did you buy?" He held up another sandwich. "You want this?" Willy shook his head no. "I'm going to see if she's up yet."

Willy balled the wax paper in his fist. "Where do you want me to start first?"

"Take your pick. The foundation people are going to be here in an hour. Do you mind working with them?"

"OK."

"Also, I can't get the sink working in the kitchen."

"I'm on it." Willy stood up and followed him into the house.

Brad crouched by the air mattress, where Julie lay peacefully sleeping. He touched her cheek gently without any response. Taking a long curl, he considered its light brown color, and he pulled the hair from last night out of his pocket. Holding it against her locks, he felt the different textures. Julie's was soft, the other brittle. While his wife's hair caught the sun in its blond depths, the red hair was duller. He rubbed the loose hair, feeling it tingle under his fingers. It dissolved into dust as he held it. He stood, brushing off his hands, watching the fine powder fall into the cracks of the weathered floorboards. He touched the cold floor, trying to sweep it up, but found nothing there. Julie stirred, smiled, and stretched until her muscles protested.

"Wow, how did I get here?" She took a deep, satisfying breath.

"How do you feel?" He turned a concerned gaze on her.

She sat up, leaning on her hands, wincing. "Ow. I fell asleep?"

"It was the drugs they gave you. You remember anything?" He studied her face, wondering if she recalled her wild behavior of the night before.

"Nothing after we left the hospital." Something dropped in the other room, and Julie jumped.

"Willy just got here. You want my phone? You have to call in sick."

Julie made a face. "I have to talk to you about that. I kind of quit my job yesterday."

Brad sat on the floor and handed her the sandwich. "What happened?"

"Mr. Wilson. He was…inappropriate."

"What do you mean, inappropriate?"

Julie shrugged, tears welling in her eyes. "He wanted to…you know."

"No, I don't know. What happened, Jules?" Brad said, his voice rising.

"He tried to touch me. He didn't. Brad, stop." She pulled him back before he could stand up. "I hit him. It's over." She caressed his tense hand.

"I'll kill him." Brad's face looked like stone.

"No, you won't. I don't work there anymore. We need the bank. I am not going to say anything; otherwise, he'll have the bank pull in our credit line."

"I'll still kill him."

Brad stood. Julie stood as well and came up behind him, feeling the intense power in his body.

"No, we are moving on. Now we really have to make this house move. Maybe you'll reconsider the bed-and-breakfast?" she asked hopefully.

Brad left the room without answering her. He found Willy under the sink, his great arms twisting a wrench.

"I know you're there. I can hear your heavy breathing." Willy laughed. "Turn on the water."

Brad walked over to the sink and turned on the faucet. The pipes gave an agonizing groan, followed by a belch and a brown trickle making its way into the dirty porcelain sink.

"The stove works. Now you have water. I'd say we are halfway there. The fridge is a goner." Willy hoisted himself up. "What's going on? I could hear you all the way in here."

"Julie's boss got too familiar with her."

"I never liked that guy. You going to do something?"

Brad looked up at him with a smirk, whispering, "Not right now."

"She OK?"

"I am fine." Julie entered, limping slightly, and walked straight into Willy's warm embrace. "How are Rita and LaMarr?"

"It's all good. I don't know, I leave for four days and come back to holy hell." He noticed a truck pulling into the back. "I think the foundation people are here. I'll see you later."

Brad looked at Julie, his hands on his hips.

"I'm crimping your style," she stated.

"You could say that," he agreed.

"I can help?" she answered.

"Not with those hands. I've got some gloves in the truck. There's a shitload of stuff in the attic. You can start going through that, as long as your hands are covered. There's, like, ten decades of junk up there."

"Yes, sir, captain, sir."

Brad pulled her into his embrace. "You scared me, Jules. I've never been so frightened in all my life."

"I'm good as new." She held up her hands. "We'll make this thing work. I have a good feeling about it."

"Now look what you've done, Ollie," Gerald told Tessa, as he kicked the balled food wrapping from the center of the room.

"Ollie? What are you talking about?" Tessa sneered.

"You know, Stan Laurel and Oliver Hardy. Don't you remember the movies from the thirties?"

"Movies! Some of us were too busy to watch shows."

Gerald laughed, "I guess when you're too busy terrorizing the humans, you don't need other entertainment." He was in charity with her once again. Gerald couldn't stay mad at her. One look at her alabaster skin, her sultry eyes, her plump cheeks, and all his resentment vanished. "Don't get all irritated with me, Tessa. You know what you did to your descendants. Drove them mad, you did. What did you do to his wife?"

"Who, Miss Mouse? Nothing." However, her smile told him it was a bit more.

"You are asking for trouble, my dear. You know the Sentinels—"

Gerald was cut off by a bloodcurdling scream from below. Brad raced right through them, leaving them spinning dizzily.

"It wasn't me!" Tessa shouted. "It wasn't me!"

Brad raced down the steps two at a time. Flashlights illuminated the subcellar. A crowd of workers surrounded a man's body splayed on the floor.

"He screamed and then just collapsed," the foreman took off his hard hat. "I'll call nine-one-one."

Brad fell to his knees beside Willy, who lay spread-eagled. His head moved, and Brad released the breath he was holding.

"Don't call nobody," Willy muttered. "They don't know we here."

"You OK, Will?"

Willy raised himself on his elbows. "The slave catcher gonna come. We have to leave here, Mistah Hemmings."

"What? What? Give him air. Anybody have a bottle of water?" A bottle of Evian was put in his hand, and Brad raised Willy's head to drink.

Willy took a swig, then coughed, spitting it out.

"What is that shit, Brad? You trying to poison me? Don't nobody got Dasani? You know how I feel about the fancy stuff."

"Wow, Willy, what happened?" Brad helped his friend sit up.

"I don't know." He looked up at the other men, who shrugged.

"All I saw was you grab your leg and go down."

Brad examined his leg. "Does it hurt? Come on, let's get you out of here." He helped him rise and then placed Willy's arm over his own shoulder. "Can you manage?"

"I'm fine, man. Let's finish the job."

Brad shook his head. "They'll finish the job without you. Come on." He helped Willy out of the space and up the stairs.

"Do you want me to call an ambulance?" the foreman called out.

Brad looked at Willy, who shook his head no.

The workers shifted uneasily. The foreman, sensing their disquiet, laughed heartily.

"Come on, fellas. This is one, two, three, and collect our money." He admitted to himself that the place gave him the creeps.

Turning in the confined space, the three workers hoisted the rotting timbers. One gasped as he dropped the boards.

"Did you see that? Did you? There's a body down there!"

Seated in the parlor, Willy drank from a bottle of less expensive water.

"It was like the walls started to close in on me. I had my hands under the support beam, and everything went blank."

"You said something about your leg," Brad told him.

"I don't remember anything."

"What about when you woke up? You talked about a Mr. Hemmings."

Willy shook his head. "I don't remember anything. Just—"

"Yeah?" Brad questioned.

"Just a feeling…a really sad feeling. Like I was trapped."

They heard the rush of pounding feet, and a fist banged the back door. Brad got up, meeting the foreman by the back porch.

"We can't do no more. You got to call the police."

"Police? Why?"

"We found a skeleton. There was a body squeezed under the house."

"Shit," Brad cursed as he dialed the cops.

CHAPTER TWELVE

1862

"You can't hide them here." Gerald grabbed Kurt by the collar.

"I'm untouchable."

"Nobody's untouchable. The slave catchers are ruthless. They'll hurt your sister."

"She doesn't know anything. I swear the family is safe. Did you hear that?"

Two sets of hooves approached the house just as the sun rose in the east. The rays slanted through the dense foliage. They heard the firm steps of someone walking on the dew-laden gravel.

Gerald struck a match, and the two men casually lit their cigars. The smoke painted their faces blue. Lewis, Gerald's cousin, walked toward them, buttoning the front of his tunic.

"Gerald." He nodded. "Kurt."

"What are you still doing here?" Gerald asked. His eyes caught the lace of Tessa's bedroom window. She peered through the glass, her negligee slightly parted. Their gazes met. Tessa stared at Gerald, a smile of contentment on her face. She had something in her hand. She snapped open the fan, languidly fanning herself. *Tessa, you are driving me crazy*, he thought. Her eyes rested on his cousin, and with a laugh she drifted away.

"I had an appointment with a lady."

He slipped a cheroot between his straight white teeth, waiting for Gerald to light it. Gerald cupped the growing flame, letting Lewis suck on the cigar until the tip glowed red.

"Three on a match is unlucky," Lewis said.

"Only on a battlefield." Gerald dropped the match and it burned out.

"What are you boys doing out back here?"

"I could ask the same of you," Hemmings replied.

"Getting some fresh air."

"The party ended hours ago, Lewis," Gerald said impatiently.

"Only for some." Lewis smiled.

The door behind them unlatched, and all three turned to see the large slave stick his head out.

"I told you to stay put," Kurt hissed.

"Cicero bad, suh. He burning up," the large black man called out.

"So blows the wind in this quarter. It's illegal to hide other people's property, Kurt, or are you so rich that you take whatever you want, regardless of ownership?"

"That's enough, Lewis. You are wearing a blue uniform; surely you understand what this is about." Gerald ground out his cigar with the pointed toe of his boot.

"I am serving in the army because your father paid me to take your place," he told Gerald.

"I joined," Gerald replied defensively. "You didn't have to."

"Your father was afraid you'd be sent to the front. He gave me five hundred dollars to take your place. When you insisted on joining up, he paid Hemmings to get you a job with McClellan. You thought he did it as a favor— hardly, Gerald. Everybody can be bought and sold. You'll never see action. Your father has your life mapped out for you. After a few years of playing soldier, you come back, marry Tessa or some other chit, and take over the family business. If I live, he's setting me up with a branch in Boston." He turned to Kurt. "You are a total surprise," he laughed.

"Please, suh. We need a doctor," the large man interrupted, his face dripping with sweat.

They heard booted feet coming up the drive.

"Get back," Kurt whispered over his shoulder.

Three bounty hunters, dirty from days on the trail, met them at the top of the drive. They were leading big roan horses and all were armed.

"We're hunting for four fugitive slaves. One female, three males. You seen 'em?" He held out papers for Kurt, who took them with authority. "We will pay for information."

Lewis's eyes gleamed in the early morning light.

"Kurt Hemmings." He introduced himself as he scanned the papers. "Surely you don't think I am hiding runaways."

"There's a safe house in the area. We know it exists. We just left the Friends Meeting House in Jericho."

"And?" Kurt looked up sharply.

"There was nothing there except a bunch of old graves. The trail led us here. It was plain as day. We can take it up with a magistrate and have the house searched."

"Why don't you do just that?" Gerald snatched the papers to hand them back. "There is nobody here."

The three men bristled, and one said, "We'd like to take a look."

"Bring the magistrate," Kurt responded. "Is that all?"

Angrily, they mounted their horses and left, the growing light allowing their eyes to search for more tracks.

Gerald turned to Kurt. "You have to get them out of here."

"Where do they go next? I'll take them," Lewis said casually, his eyes silvered with greed.

Gerald knew he'd turn them over for the reward.

Kurt shook his head. "It's my responsibility. I can't let anyone else do it."

"Your father is leaving. You have a house full of people. It will raise questions as to your whereabouts."

"No, I'll take them." Gerald turned to Lewis. "Alone."

Lewis shrugged. "Makes no difference to me." He pivoted abruptly, leaving them.

Somehow, Gerald knew, it made a difference—a big difference.

Kurt pulled a crumpled map from his pocket. "We have to risk you taking them now. We can't wait for tonight. The next stop is Binghamton, the Zion Baptist

Church up there. The deacon is a station master. Once they get upstate, he'll get them to Canada. I don't know how we are going to move the wounded man."

As it turned out, it didn't matter. He had died a few minutes earlier. The girl sat on the dirt floor, crying over her brother's body. They descended into the gloom of the subcellar.

"He's dead," the girl wailed.

"You have to leave. Now." Kurt raised her up. "Go with my friend. He will get you to the next station."

"My brother?" She looked back at his body.

"Will stay here. You can't travel with his body. I will take care of it. Go. Now."

They left. Kurt wrapped the body in sailcloth. He rolled the young slave under the foundation of the house, watching silently as his body was absorbed by the darkness.

From the front porch, Lewis watched the slave catchers leave. He turned to the stable hand and ordered that his horse be brought from the stable. He mounted it, his eyes roving to Tessa's bedroom window. She was watching him, a smile on her lips, Gerald's closed fan in her hand. In the age-old language of flirtation, she opened it and started fanning herself slowly, letting him know she wasn't interested in him. When their eyes met, she sped up, her smile sultry. Her mind was changing, and she was telling him. She deliberately snapped it shut, smacking her palm impatiently. She wanted him; the message was clear. Her intent was written in her next action. She rubbed it up and down, then put it against her lips. He smiled, tipped his hat, and blew her a kiss. He would be back for her, and they would finish the silent conversation she had started.

Gerald watched Tessa tease his cousin, the fan he bought her now a weapon stabbing him in his heart. Why couldn't she see how he felt about her?

Kurt stood next to him and whispered, "She's a faithless jade."

"She's your sister," Gerald replied.

"That doesn't change the fact that she has the morality of a whore."

Gerald grabbed Kurt by the lapels, pushing him against the wall of the house. "Don't talk about her like that."

"You should move on, Gerry. She's not for you. Tessa belongs to no one. You'll never satisfy her, and she'll break your heart."

Gerald released Kurt with a sigh of resignation. "I don't have one anymore. She destroyed it years ago."

"You could marry her—I know that's what my father wants—but you'll never possess her soul."

"Can anyone ever possess someone's soul?"

"She's controlling yours," Kurt stated.

"Do you think I invite this torment? You think I want this? I can't tell my heart where to love. My brain knows she doesn't love me, but my heart has a will of its own."

"That may be so, Gerald. Love is for poets."

"Hah, you are a poet." Gerald laughed.

"No, I am not. I am a realist. I use whatever artifices I need to fulfill my destiny. I will marry Lady Pamela, but not because I love her. I will marry her because it will put me in an office in the government. Between her influence and my father's money, I will define my life. I will live it on my terms and not the dictates of my heart."

"I pity you. I would rather experience the limits of hope and despair rather than a cold, clinical existence where you never feel the depths of passion. Tessa will be mine. If it takes forever, she will be mine."

"You're the poet, Gerald. I hope you don't waste your life on her."

"How could anything like love be considered a waste?" Gerald shook his head. "I'll be back by tomorrow."

The wagon Kurt had arranged for had been brought to the entrance of the drive, the runaway slaves hiding under a tarp.

CHAPTER THIRTEEN

"**Y**ou're sure you don't want to go to the emergency room?" Brad repeated one more time.

"I got bumped worse on the head in Afghanistan. Stop. What did they find?"

"I'll tell you after I find Jules." Brad took the stairs two at a time until he reached the ladder to the attic. "Jules? Jules!" he called out.

"Here," she replied, turning to face him with a beaming smile. "This place is unbelievable. I can't wait to hear what Sal has to say. He may even want to do an estate sale just for all this."

Weak sunlight filtered in through a tiny window near the roof of the attic. Julie's face was framed by a huge red hat, a bright ostrich feather wrapping her cheek charmingly. The sun bathed her in a reddish hue, and Brad blinked for a moment. She appeared taller, her breasts larger, her hips wider. Even her voice seemed deeper. Squinting, he scanned the room, his gaze coming to rest again on his diminutive wife, who seemed to have shrunk, looking like a child trying on play clothes.

"Whoa, slow down. We have a bit of a problem."

Julie pulled off the hat she was wearing and walked toward him. "What's the matter?"

"Well, they found a body—"

"What?" she shrieked. "Where? Eww!"

"Not quite a body. Bones. We have to call in the police. We won't be able to do much of anything until they green-light us."

"Oh my God." Julie sank down on a rickety chair.

Brad got down on one knee and took her hands in his. "You're supposed to be wearing gloves." He examined the dirty bandages. Julie shrugged. "I don't want you to get an infection." He kissed the dirty palms of her hands.

Julie pulled his face against her chest, resting her head on top of his. "Who do you think it is?"

"I don't know, but the police will want to investigate. They'll be here in a few. Come downstairs. We'll talk to them and then we need to make a run to Target."

"Target?"

"Jules, you don't even have a phone anymore. We need a few changes of clothes, shoes—earth to Julie—we need a few basics. My stuff burned up, too. Are you still woozy?" He searched her face with concern.

"Don't be silly. I'm fine." Julie playfully held his face in her hands. "There is a ton of late nineteenth-century and early twentieth-century clothing up here if you're interested. I've been playing *Downton Abbey* for the last hour."

"Jules, our home burned down. You don't have a job. Are you sure you're OK?"

Julie stood, her hand caressing a rack with period clothes hanging from it. "It was covered with dust cloths," she told him. "Everything's been preserved, like it's been waiting for us. I don't know, Brad. I feel like I am finally home."

"Well," he said, as he rose from his knees, "don't get too comfortable. We're going to need a lot of money to get ourselves back to where we have to be. We have miles to go before we get to our destination."

Julie watched him leave the attic, thinking she was sure they had arrived at their destination.

CHAPTER FOURTEEN

Detective Chambers and his partner were in the main salon when Julie came down. They were taking a statement from the foreman of the foundation workers. Then they quizzed both Brad and Julie about buying the house, asking dozens of questions.

"Well," the detective said, as he closed his notebook, "the bones look like they've been there for a while. The crime lab will be here later today."

"You mean like *CSI?*" Willy asked.

"Yeah, just like on television. Don't do any work back there for now."

"We are on a tight schedule, Detective Chambers. When you do a flip, moving it fast is vital. Oh, crap!" Brad cursed when a News 12 van pulled up to the house. "Who called them?"

"They follow our bulletins. You can't hide from the press."

Brad cursed again, long and fluently. "This is going to devalue the house."

"Not if we turn it into a haunted bed-and-breakfast."

Brad spun on her, his face taut with anxiety. "Julie, stop that already. We are moving the house as soon as we get a buyer."

Julie paled, embarrassed by his outburst. She opened her mouth to say something, then pressed her lips into a thin white line.

They left Willy working on stripping wallpaper in the center hallway. Wordlessly, Julie hobbled to the cab of Brad's truck. "Don't ever talk to me like that again." Her tone was one of controlled rage.

"Then don't keep nagging, Julie. It ain't going to happen if you keep bothering me with it." He looked at her feet. "What are you using for shoes?"

"I found an old pair of your flip-flops in the back of the truck." She showed him her small feet in the oversized sandals. "Since when do you make all the decisions?"

"Since when do you?" Brad shot back.

Brad backed out of the driveway, causing a female reporter and her camera crew crossing the gravel to scatter. He heard her call out to him, "Mr. Evans. Brad and Julie Evans? Do you want to make a statement?" The reporter was younger than Julie, with long brown hair and a dark trench coat.

"Are you going to stop?" Julie asked icily.

Brad didn't answer as he shifted the car into drive and hit the gas, barely missing the cameraman who was intent on filming the two of them. "I don't owe them anything. Nothing good is going to come out of this."

"They're going to knock on the door," Julie said as they barreled down the street.

"Oh, I think Willy will handle them fine," Brad said grimly.

They spent the next hour in Target in stony silence. Julie was able to stock up on basic groceries. Brad picked up a counter-sized fridge and made sure he got enough beer to fill it. It was looking to be a long evening ahead of them. Brad refused to let her load the car, making her take a seat while he packed up their supplies.

"Look," she said, as he lifted himself into his seat, "I don't want to fight with you. In fact, I don't know why I am."

Brad groaned. "It's like you're someone else or something, Jules." He leaned over to kiss her gently on the lips. "Just stop. We'll figure it out. I promise you."

His phone rang, and Brad pressed the button. Sal's greeting filled the car.

"Where are you? You didn't show up yesterday."

"Long story," Brad said.

"Yeah, really long," Julie added.

"Hi, Julie. I have some time today. I'll swing by around four. Will you still be at the Bedlam House then?"

"Yeah, we'll be there," Brad responded.

They got back with lunch to hear a rich baritone filling the house. "Swing low, sweet chariot, comin' for to carry me home. Swing low, sweet chariot, coming for to carry me home. I looked over Jordan, and what did I see—"

"Willy? Will, is that you?" Brad called out.

They found him on his hands and knees, scrubbing the floor.

"What the heck are you singing?" The words died in Brad's throat when Willy looked at him, his eyes a fiery red. "Oh shit!" He dropped the bag he was carrying, eggs slamming onto the floor.

"Whatsa matter with you?" Willy lumbered to his feet.

Julie cried out, "Brad!"

"I just finished that part of the floor."

"Willy?" Brad took a deep breath. "You OK?"

"Are you?" Willy asked him with annoyance.

They carried the bags into the kitchen, which had been put in some semblance of order by Willy. Brad started taking out cans and packages of food from the bags and putting them on the countertop. Julie ran her hand appreciatively across its pitted surface.

"Did you see anything strange when we walked in? Jules," he urged, "did you?"

"Um, no…why?"

"I…nothing. You didn't see anything?"

"Brad, what are you talking about? Isn't this counter beautiful?"

"It's all abused and tired-looking. Hey, how come our old countertop was a mess and this one is just as bad, but you think it's OK?"

"This one is an antique. It has character."

"Are you kidding me? It's junk."

"You can't tell me what to like and what not to like!" Julie rounded on him with hostility.

"Cool your jets, Jules. I'm just making an observation."

Julie sniffed loudly, ignoring his last remark, and turned her back to put the rest of the food away in silence.

Brad walked into the parlor to find Willy giving him the silent treatment, too, while he cleaned up the broken eggs. Brad heard him humming the old slave song again, sending chills dancing up his spine.

"Will. Willy."

"Yeah?"

"You feel strange?"

"Nah. Why?"

Brad cleared his throat. "You're acting kinda strange."

Willy shrugged. "I wouldn't talk if I were you. You as nervous as a tick on a bull."

"A tick on a bull? What the heck are you talking about? Willy, did you hit your head?"

Willy took the rag he was using to clean up the broken eggs and threw it, hard, hitting Brad in the center of his chest. "Clean up your own damn mess." He stalked out of the room.

Brad looked down at the dripping yolk on his shirt, wondering what was going on in this house. Why were they all fighting with one another?

Sal hopped up the steps to the house a few minutes later. "What a dump." He reached out to shake Brad's hand.

"My sentiments exactly." Brad frowned. "Julie's in love with the place."

"You can't tell a heart where to love." Sal shrugged. "Nice chandelier." He pointed to the many-armed lighting fixture in the salon. "I could resell it."

Brad looked up. "I don't want to strip the house. We'll have to replace those things. We've got these boxes." He laid a hand on the shortest of the many stacks. "I'll ask Jules to go up to the attic with you. I think at this point, you should take it all to your place and go through the boxes there."

"Sure, whatever you need. Hey, buddy, what's wrong?"

Brad shuffled his feet. "This place. It's strange."

"Depressing."

"More than that. All we do is fight. Julie's, like, obsessed with the house."

"Women," Sal observed.

Brad nodded as if that explained everything.

Tessa took this moment to rub up against Sal. He was a chubby one. She wrapped her arms around his thick middle, running her agile hands up and down his sides. The large man shivered, making a guttural sound that stopped Brad in his tracks.

"What's the matter?"

Sal shook his head like a dog. "This place is creepy. I felt like someone was dancing on my grave."

"Dancing on a grave!" Tessa shrieked, flying into a rage.

Gerald laughed from his seat on the chandelier where he observed her failed seduction. "Looks like you're losing your touch."

"Oh, you think so?" She flew up to him, her face purple with anger. "Watch this."

She spun down to come up against Brad. Her long arms started to encircle him, when a darkness fell across the room. Both men looked up, seeing nothing but feeling the oppressive presence. Tessa felt the power of the Sentinels as they gathered her none too gently and removed her from the room.

"Feels like all the air got sucked out of the room," Sal said as he glanced around.

"You felt that, too?" Brad met his eyes. He had a ringing in his ears. He noticed Sal had stuck his pinky into his own ear and was shaking it.

Sal gulped. "Weird, right?"

"Like we're on the set of *Dark Shadows* or something."

"*Dark Shadows.* Brad, man, you're funny."

"Yeah, a regular barrel of laughs," Brad agreed grimly.

Julie relieved Brad to help Sal go through the boxes in the attic. She was strangely subdued, and Brad was worried about her. He stopped every so often, just to look at her white face.

"You're sure you're OK?"

"I told you I'm fine!" she snapped.

"Hands sore? Ankle OK?"

"I'll let you know if they're not," Julie said impatiently.

"Forgive me for caring," Brad retorted, but really what he thought was, *Well, screw you, too.* He jumped down from the ladder, calling out, "If you need me, I'll be working in the dining room."

"What's the matter with you two—honeymoon over?" Sal laughed. "Hey, Julie, that doll, hand it here."

Julie held up a doll she had taken out of faded tissue paper. "Catch."

She hefted it, and Sal screamed, "No! It's porcelain. Hand and feet intact. Mint condition."

"I'm only kidding. What's it worth?"

"Two grand, no sweat. It's German."

Julie looked at the doll in its nineteeth-century gown, a lovely taffeta, complete with a reticule and tiny booted feet. "She is beautiful. Maybe I'll keep her."

"You want to keep everything," Sal laughed.

"Yes, she does, but it's mine," Tessa said morosely.

The Sentinels had deposited her there, thankfully. It was a sight better than their usual place. She was seated glumly in an old rocker. Watching the young woman touch all her things gave her the chills. Talk about feeling like someone was dancing on your grave. She began rocking, humming a waltz, the chair swaying in time to the melody.

Julie stopped what she was doing, looked up, and saw the rocker moving back and forth. Her fascinated gaze traveled to the side of the chair, settling on an abandoned ladies' fan. She walked to it and reached down to grab it, when a force slammed into her while a very feminine scream of "Mine!" echoed in her head. She landed hard on her hip, the wind knocked out of her.

"You OK, kiddo? Maybe you're not ready for all this work." Sal looked up at her over the rims of his bifocals.

"Did you hear anything?" She looked at Sal.

"Just your ass hitting the floor. Take a break. I'll get my guys up here to start loading. I think you're going to make a nice few bucks, Julie. The china alone is worth about ten grand. It's a complete set of Wedgwood. There're fifty place settings. There must have been some gigantic parties here at one time."

"I think he was a railroad baron or something. I keep meaning to google Hemmings, but alas"—she held the fan to her head dramatically, then fanned herself furiously—"I don't have a laptop anymore." Julie fluttered her eyelashes, her gaze cloyingly sweet.

"She doesn't even know how to do it!" Tessa sneered, her eyes glowing red.

Tessa, wild with fury, watched the girl paw through her possessions. Floating around the room, she spun faster and faster as her agitation rose. With dizzying speed, she banged into Julie again, her laughter bouncing off the wooden walls. Julie swayed, feeling dizzy. Maybe she *was* working too hard.

Sal took a call and told her, "My guys just got here. They'll take over. Sit down and let them cart this stuff out of here."

Julie sat on the rocker, holding the pretty doll, letting the peace of the moment wash through her. The fan hung on her delicate wrist as though it belonged there. Two workers started carrying out the boxes, and soon all she saw was the dust motes drifting in the weak sunlight coming through the strangely shaped windows. Builders called them eyebrows because usually a house had two of them in the vicinity of the attic. They even looked like eyebrows on the front of the house. Resting her head against the wicker of the chair, she rocked gently, lost in thought. Her eyes drifted shut. Minutes later, she felt the momentum change. The rocker moved faster, its curved wooden rails lifting higher and higher. Her hands gripped the arms, her feet trying to stop it, the movement slamming her hard against the medallion back of the rocker. She opened her mouth to call Brad, when abruptly the air was sucked from her lungs. Her face purpling, Julie gasped for air; her chest felt as though an elephant were sitting on it. Her arms were plastered to her sides, held by invisible shackles. Wheezing, she tried to squeeze air into her lungs, her eyesight becoming pinpoints of white light. Just as suddenly as it had started, relief came. In an instant, the pressure was gone. Julie pulled great gulps of air into her starved lungs, her eyes tearing, her hands suddenly free to stop the manic rocking of the chair.

She stood on shaky legs, looking around the room. The porcelain doll lay broken in a heap on the dirty floor, the beautiful face cracked in half. Julie whimpered as she bent to pick it up, her eyes cautiously darting around the layered shadows of the room.

This time when the Sentinels removed Tessa, she was put in the very dark place she didn't like.

Gerald went after her, sharing her imprisonment despite her resentful silence. Tessa shook her foot impatiently, her eyes scanning the deep cavern.

"How long do you think they'll keep us here?"

Gerald shrugged. It was devoid of noise, an airless space, with no walls to confine them, yet Tessa was confined.

"I said, how long do you think they'll keep us here?" she demanded.

"I don't know, Tessa. I don't communicate with them. They don't tell me their plans. They just do. This is what happens when you cause trouble."

"What's that supposed to mean?"

"It means"—Gerald stood to float around the blank space—"that I never have a problem with them."

"Because you're invisible." Tessa flicked a red-gold lock of hair defiantly. "You were invisible while you were alive, and you're just as invisible now that you're dead."

Gerald grabbed Tessa by her arms. They levitated, their feet dangling, weightless in space. Tessa rigidly pulled away, but Gerald gripped her chin, kissing her in a combustible mixture of frustration, anger, and finally his devastating love. Tessa fought him, her hands pushing at his shoulders.

"Get away from me!" she shouted. Tessa shoved him with both hands. "I can't stand you. No matter how much you wait, I'll never love you. You can't make me love you. I wish you weren't here. I want a real man, even if he's dead. I want one who makes me feel like a woman," she told him, aiming all her resentment toward his ever-ready shoulders. Usually, he would soothe her, try to negotiate to get her out of there.

Gerald backed up, his chest heaving. "Have it your way, Tessa. I have waited long enough for you." He winked out, and she was left with blankness.

Tessa blinked into the darkness. Nothing but the blackness stared back at her. She could hear the jumbled thoughts in her head. She floated, her hands splayed, sometimes spinning into an aimless vortex and rotating until she lost all her bearings. It was so quiet it hurt; the lack of light hurt, the loneliness hurt. He had left her. She had finally pushed him far enough, and Gerald, who had said he'd never leave her, had simply abandoned her to this void. It was cold. She was freezing. There was no one to comfort her.

Reaching out, she called, "Gerald? Gerald?" She drifted; there was nothing to latch on to, an absence of light, the silence of the vacuum filling her head. Tessa was alone. Completely and utterly alone. "Gerrrrald!" she screamed into the darkness.

Willy left when the sun set, his good humor restored with the promise of breakfast and his return the next morning. He had made short work of the reporter and her crew. He recounted the story to Brad; it was a simple matter of confusing doublespeak. Frustrated, they left, vowing to return. The forensics guys came and went, taking the bag of bones for study. They told Willy the bones were really old, maybe a hundred years or more. The thighbone was broken, a lead ball nearby. This confirmed the remains were from the last century. A report would follow, they promised. Brad, Julie, and Willy could work on the house, but they had to stay out of the subcellar until the case was closed. Willy waited until they were alone before handing Brad a huge machete.

"What's this for?" Brad held up the deadly knife.

"There's some bad mojo here. I don't know, brother, but you got to be prepared."

Brad considered the weapon. "You're not buying into any ghost crap, are you, Will?"

"Let me just say that this place gives me the willies." He laughed. "So I think I got to give a little Willy's back."

Brad stuck the large knife in a corner of the main salon, behind boxes of bottled water. He then stepped out onto the porch, looking to make sure no reporters were camped out on the street. Briefly, he thought of brandishing the machete, just to get a rise out of the reporters. He smiled evilly, thinking of the pleasure of screwing with them, but it seemed they had finally given up. Satisfied that they were alone, he shut off the outdoor lights and locked the large double doors with a strange feeling of domesticity. He walked through the house, turning off lights, finally coming into the main salon that was serving as their bedroom. The fire he'd lit earlier warmed the room with a honey hue. Julie was fast asleep, a half-empty glass of milk next to her on the floor.

Silently, Brad stripped, sliding in beside Julie's sleeping form. He noticed the fan lying on the bed beside her face. It was a queen-size mattress, large enough to make each feel lonely on his or her side. The house settled, and with a strange feeling of ownership, Brad identified the squeaks and rattles he was beginning to recognize. Pipes clanged, radiators hissed, and he watched his wife's hunched shoulders. Scooting over, he spooned with her. Julie wiggled against him, letting him feel right at home. She turned into his embrace, fitting neatly under his chin, with a satisfied sigh of relief. He looked down and saw that her eyes were open. They glittered in the darkness. She held the fan above them and expertly snapped it open, the fretwork of the spines letting in the moonlight from the window. She stared at the painting of the Asian ladies, touching the images with her forefinger.

"It's pretty," she whispered.

Brad kissed her and rumbled, "Like its new owner."

Julie snuggled into him, the fan slipping to the floor beside the bed. Sleep gentled them, Brad's soft snores comforting Julie while she rested. Their arms twined, and when their eyes opened, both reflected a red glow.

Gerald blinked in surprise, taking in a deep breath, his lungs filling with air. It bubbled in his chest, his nostrils flaring. His eyes widened as he lifted his hands to stare at the pads of his fingertips, then caressed the velvet softness of the body next to him. Gerald touched his lips against Tessa's startled mouth, as if asking permission. She made a sound between a whimper and a whisper, but he heard her say yes. Tessa's fingers stroked his hair, creating rivulets of shivering pleasure. She held her body against his, drinking in the contact, her hands embracing his back so that they touched everywhere. He heard her murmur, her deep voice vibrating against his chest, the whisper of her breath feathering across his collarbone. He knew he spoke but couldn't remember what he said, as his mouth traveled over her petal-soft flesh. She was all rose and milk, her flesh vibrant and alive, her body responding to his touch with delight. He pressed his nose to the soft skin between her shoulder and neck, drinking the dewy moistness that pearled on its surface. Tessa gasped with wonder, opening her body without reservation, the sensual delight of flesh against flesh awakening ancient memories. She placed their hands palm to palm, open and defenseless, completely giving herself to him. Their bodies touched again and again, feverishly reaching new heights, not wanting the night to end. Both exhaled in an explosion of pleasure; Gerald's borrowed heart beat furiously in his chest. Slick with sweat, he lay still, holding Tessa, who clung to his wide shoulders, a single tear escaping her luminous eyes.

"I thought you left me," she whispered with a sob.

Gerald shook his head mutely.

"I was afraid. I don't want to be alone," she whispered close to his ear.

Gerald planted his lips over hers, kissing her gently, using Brad's body to wrap himself around her. They touched everywhere. His fingers grazed her swollen lips.

"I am tired of waiting," he told her.

"Then don't wait anymore."

Gerald closed his eyes with pleasure, his hands cupping Tessa's full breasts, relief warring with excitement. Tessa's experienced hands caressed him, snatching the breath from his body, sending chills down his torso. It felt so good. He whispered how much he loved her, taking what she offered. Tessa loved him back the way he'd always dreamed. They rocked together, locked in a timeless dance, their eyes lighting with deep passion, making them blind to everything but the intensity of their borrowed time. Spent and replete, Tessa touched Gerald's cheek, her gaze thoughtful as she considered his smooth skin. Gerald opened his mouth to speak, and she silenced him with a kiss.

Brad woke to stare at his wife's naked form in his arms. Did he dream that they had made love? His body told him it was no dream, but the memory was hazy. Pulling her close, he kissed her again, making sure the memories he created next would be his own.

CHAPTER FIFTEEN

1862

Tessa raced down the stairs, her dress unfastened in the rear, her hair a mass of red-gold tangles. Dawn poked over the water, painting the calm bay orange and gold. She ran to the front door to see Gerald turning from their drive onto Bedlam, the cumbersome wagon swaying on the rutted road. She opened her mouth to call him back, but the words died in her throat. She never thanked him for the fan. She watched the wagon's slow progress down the road beside the water. She wanted to tell him something. She wasn't sure just what, but it gnawed at her consciousness.

"He's not going to wait around for you forever, you know."

Kurt came up behind her, resting his tall, lanky frame against the fretted post supporting the porch roof. He chewed on the end of a cheroot, the acidic smell burning her nose. Tessa made a face.

"Oh yes, he will," she told her brother with conviction. "He'll never leave me."

"There will come a day he'll be tired of your behavior. Then where will you be?"

"Make sure Lady Pamela loves you more than you love her," Tessa told him, her eyes watching the diminishing figure in the wagon.

"Why?"

"I thought you were a poet, Kurt. Don't you know the one who commands a heart wins?" She opened the fan, hiding her lower face, her eyes coming to rest on the lone figure of a soldier leaning against the fence post. "No one will ever command me. I own my own heart." She fanned herself, a languid smile inviting Lewis to come back to the house.

CHAPTER SIXTEEN

"**B**rad." Julie looked up from Brad's laptop. Hers had been destroyed in the fire, and Brad had given her the one he kept in the truck. She sat cross-legged on their air mattress. "There's some weird shit happening in this house."

Brad dropped the towel that was around his waist. He stood in all his naked glory, and Julie snapped the computer lid closed to drink in his maleness.

"I thought it was rather conservative sex this morning. Nary a handcuff in sight."

Julie blushed. "I'm not talking about that. There is definitely something odd about this place."

Brad agreed as he slid on his jeans. "So?"

"So...there is this woman. Her name is"—she consulted the laptop again—"Georgia Oaken. She talks to dead people."

"Stop right there, partner. No exorcisms allowed. The only things I saw spinning last night were stars." He stooped to kiss her. His breath smelled of toothpaste and coffee.

She pulled his head down. "Please?"

Brad shook his head. "Waste of time, waste of money. I'm beginning to appreciate the old house, Jules. If we share it with a bunch of shades, it makes no difference to me."

"But what if they are interfering? Brad, I really think we should consider it."

"Not gonna happen," he told her, as he walked out of the room to start the day's project.

Julie looked down at the laptop, reading testimonials about the psychic. She clicked on the link to a new book Oaken had just published, buying it on Amazon. She heard Willy's voice from the other room, so she got up, dressed, and wandered in to where they were consulting a punch list.

"We're going to Home Depot," Brad said without looking up. "Are you sure these are the colors you want for the master bath?"

"I like them."

"I didn't ask if you like them, I asked if you're sure you want them."

Julie bristled. What was wrong with him now? Just because she'd brought up a psychic, his mood had soured. She saw Willy roll his eyes.

"What do you think, Will?"

"Not getting involved with your domestic crap. What's going on with you two?"

"Nothing." Brad folded the paper and walked out the door. He stopped at the entrance and turned to Willy. "You coming or what?"

Willy stood slowly, looked at the two of them, and shook his head. He grumbled something under his breath, turned to Julie, and said, "What side of the bed did he get out of?"

She shrugged, annoyed with Brad. "Who knows? He was fine last night." A memory of it rushed back at her, and for a moment her jaw dropped. "He's just not himself," she whispered, and then gulped.

Willy headed outside and hopped into the cab of Brad's pickup. At the end of the long driveway, he asked, "What's that all about, man?"

"What?" Brad pulled out onto Bedlam Street. "Shit, I forgot. I have to get something to Sal. Mind if we make a stop by his place first?"

"What's going on between you and Julie?"

"I don't know. Lately, she's turned into a nag. She'd better get busy pretty soon."

"I hear you. What she want?"

"She wants to bring in a psychic to talk to the spirits in the house."

Willy laughed so hard tears ran down his face. "You kidding me. Who she want, that white lady on TV?"

"How'd you know?"

"She's young, Brad. She never saw the shit we saw in her life. She's a kid. Maybe you should humor her."

"No way. It's a crock, and we don't have any money to waste."

They pulled up to Sal's antique shop. Sal was in the rear of the dimly lit store. He looked up when they knocked, running to unlock the door and let them in.

"You're up early," he told them, as they walked to counter in the back of the cluttered store. "You've got a major haul in that house. You might have hit a little jackpot."

"Don't tell Julie," Brad said morosely. He was carrying a box, which he set on the high counter. "She wants to turn it into a bed-and-breakfast."

"Really?" Sal asked. Brad and Julie were solid partners in both marriage and business.

"She's just so damn strange about that house. The sooner we flip it, the better."

Sal looked up questioningly; he was trying to glue a flower onto the dress of a china figurine.

"She wants to hire that television psychic to talk to our ghosts."

The three men laughed.

"Who, you mean Georgia?" Sal said. "She wants Georgia Oaken?"

"You've heard of her?"

"Who hasn't?" He shrugged and went back to his tinkering. "She did a job for the Realtor next door. One of the old estates he was selling was purportedly haunted. She cleansed it for them. That's how she met Molly." He paused to look over his shoulder. "She asked Molly to run her appointment books. Molly works for her at night."

"Molly? The girl you've been dating?"

"Woman. Yeah, we met at Georgia's lecture. It was fate," Sal said dramatically. "Fate and Bon Jovi. She's a real fan. I took her to Jones Beach—"

"But what about the witch?" Willy interrupted.

"Medium. She's a medium. She communicates with the dead. I find her fascinating." Sal held up the broken shepherdess he was fixing. "She was speaking at the library last year. Look, see this figurine? It's about two hundred years old. Think of all the things these little eyes have seen."

"That ain't real; it can't see nothing," Willy said with a laugh.

"Well, sure. It's not real, but does it have an energy? I have been interested in antiques all my life. I think about all the people who have used the objects. How many happy or sad occasions their belongings have been through. Do these things retain something of their owners?" He held up the figure, its face staring blankly at them. "Did this object play a role in somebody's life? Is the essence of an owner imprinted on his belongings?"

"That's some deep shit, Sal, man." Willy picked up an old dueling pistol, the mechanism frozen. He hefted it, put it back, and then opened a small shaving case, touching all the bottles. "You mean like all this stuff has ghostly DNA or something?"

Brad took the porcelain shepherdess and studied the folds of her dress. He shook his head. "When a person dies, he's gone forever. I've seen enough death to know the difference."

"Maybe so, maybe not," Sal told him. "You should speak to Georgia. I could call Molly and ask her to arrange a session."

"No, thanks." He handed the figurine back to Sal. "This is the lampshade I've been meaning to give you." Gingerly, he took it out of the beat-up box. Holding it with two hands, he displayed it for Sal.

"Wow, oh wow." Sal held out eager hands to examine the colorful shade. He turned it on the side, the small mosaics of glass rattling gently. "This is the holy grail, my friend." He whistled. "It's signed. This is going to be worth some serious money, Brad."

"Well, that's good news, and I'm not sharing it with any dead people."

"What's a thing like that worth?" Willy asked.

Sal opened his laptop.

"What you doing?" Willy asked.

"I'm typing in a description. These are lotus flowers. It's signed by Louis Comfort Tiffany. It's mint, but it's just a shade, not the whole lamp. Holy crap!"

"What?" Brad asked.

"Holy crap!" Sal repeated. "I can't sell this, Brad."

"It's not stolen. I'm sure it comes from the house."

"It's not that—I have to put it in a special auction. It says here that last year a Tiffany lotus lamp sold for seven figures."

"What?"

"It sold for over a million dollars."

Brad threw his head back and roared with laughter.

CHAPTER SEVENTEEN

J ulie started demolition on a bathroom in one of the many bedrooms. She needed to lose herself in some work. She was losing her mind. Images of last night with her husband played like a movie in her head. The bodies were familiar, yet at the same time, they were not. The whole episode had a dreamlike quality, and for now, Julie wasn't sure what part of what they had done was real or from her imagination. It was better to keep busy, think about things to keep her occupied, so her head wouldn't explode.

She trudged upstairs and started working in the first of the guest bedrooms. It was an en suite, perfect for a bed-and-breakfast. Why couldn't Brad see that? she wondered. She lifted out the toilet, carefully pulled a rusty medicine cabinet from the wall, and started chopping at tiles on the floor, both of her tiny hands whacking away with a giant mallet. They had decided that nothing was salvageable in this bath. She dragged the fixtures out of the small bathroom to a cleared corner in the bedroom. It was hot. Sweat trickled down her back. She was wearing an oversized T-shirt and yoga pants from Target. She fanned herself, smiling when she thought of the pretty ladies' fan in her makeshift bedroom. Julie went to the window. The trees surrounding the house were painted amber, red, and yellow. A breeze ruffled the branches, and Julie wanted to air out the stuffy room. She pounded the painted window lock and used a screwdriver to chip away the many coats of paint crusted over it. She blew away the paint shavings, slid open the mechanism, and unlocked the window to allow a blast of cool air to circulate the room. The old sash stopped midway, frozen in place. The window wouldn't budge. Julie put her back into it, tugging at the stubborn sash, a smile lighting her face when it finally gave, allowing her to open it all the way.

She leaned on the sill, inhaling the crisp air. Stretching, she leaned out the window, drawing great gulps of fresh air and enjoying the breeze. She heard the window move and realized it was coming down fast. Falling backward, she made it in just as the sash slammed shut with a loud crack. Julie sat on the floor studying the closed window and then got up to attempt to lift it again. It was stuck fast.

Using her screwdriver, she was trying to leverage it open when the door to the bedroom slammed shut with a bang. Julie dropped the screwdriver and turned to face the door; a dart of apprehension traveled up her spine. The moment took her back to the house fire, so she nervously ran to the door, trying unsuccessfully to pry it open. The handle slid between her fingers. Panic made her heart race. She tugged at the knob, but it remained solidly shut. Julie felt the blood rush to her face, her breath quickening.

She returned to pull at the sash, attempting to open the window. She struggled with the stubborn wood, but as soon as she got it slightly raised, it slammed shut. Her nail broke down to the quick and she cursed loudly. She stuck her thumb into her mouth and then ran back to the door to try to open it. Bracing her feet, she twisted the knob, registering that it wasn't budging and that she was caught in a cosmic tug-of-war. Sweat beaded her brow, and she dug in with both bare feet to anchor herself against the force holding the door shut. She yanked hard. The door gave, propelling her to the far wall. She hit it with her back, getting the wind knocked out of her. Julie slid to the floor gasping in pain, her brain in a daze.

She put her hand beneath her to stand up, but felt a weight settle on her shoulders and hold her down. She tried to call for help, but her voice wouldn't cooperate. When it returned, it came out thin and reedy, as though she were being strangled. The door slammed shut so hard that the chandelier overhead swayed as if in an earth-quake, sending a rain of broken crystals whipping around the room. Julie felt the sting of one slicing her cheek; tears mixed with blood when she wiped her wet face. She rolled onto her stomach, coming face-to-face with the cracked medicine cabinet she had removed earlier. It lay on its side, the warped mirror reflecting her stark white face. She touched her bloody cheek, a scream dying in her throat as the image wavered. A stranger stared back at her. She touched the red-haired girl in the reflection, feeling her hand on her own face. Familiar hands touched a stranger's face, yet she was in front of a mirror.

"No," she whispered. "What do you want?" The girl in the mirror smiled back at her, making chills dance down Julie's spine. She skittered away in disbelief, her breathing shallow. "Brad," she croaked. "Help me, Brad."

The solid walls of the room looked liquid. The faded wallpaper rippled, the shape of a woman's body filling its contours. Like an ancient bas-relief, the surface filled out with a female form. The eyes opened and looked at Julie, the mouth yawning in a wordless scream.

Julie rose unsteadily, running to the door. This time it opened easily, and she raced down the stairs screaming for Brad. Julie made a beeline to the kitchen, where Brad and Willy were stacking boxes.

"I hate this place," she said as she rushed into the room. "It's possessed. We have to get out." She was panting, her eyes wild.

Brad looked up, laughing, his eyes reflecting red.

Julie screamed and ran from the house—barefoot, without a coat, and in total terror.

CHAPTER EIGHTEEN

"What was that about?" Willy looked up, shocked. "Damned if I know. Jules! Jules, come back."

Brad ran after her, but didn't see her anywhere. He stood on the porch, his eyes scanning the tangled lawn, looking for his wife. Cursing, he took the truck and circled the area. She didn't have a cell phone, or shoes, or a jacket—nothing. Where could she go? What the hell was the matter with her? He circled for hours, losing a full day of work. He called Willy several times, but Julie had not returned. He combed the narrow country roads, looking up windy driveways for his errant wife. He considered calling the police—to report what? His wife freaked out and ran half-dressed from the house. No, he figured he'd save her the embarrassment.

Julie ran down Bedlam Street, slipping, her feet frozen from the cold asphalt. She wiped the stinging cut on her cheek with the bottom of her oversized shirt. A little cottage housing a ladies' clothing store stood in a cramped row of charming pastel-colored shingled shops on the main street of the village. It was the first building she ducked into.

The interior was overbearingly warm and smelled strangely of wood smoke. It was an old building, one of the earliest restored in the town.

"May I help you?" a blue-haired lady wearing a Lilly Pulitzer lime-green sweater set inquired.

"I locked myself out of the house. I was sweeping, you know." Julie improvised with a pretend broom, a smile pasted on her face. "Could I use your phone?"

A relieved look replaced the frown on the older woman's face. "Of course, dearie. And no shoes, oh my."

Julie ignored her and dialed her sister. "Heather, I need you. Now. I am at..." She looked inquiringly at the hovering woman, who appeared interested in her conversation.

"The Perfect Fit," the woman supplied. "Bedlam and Horatio Streets."

"Thanks. Did you hear that? No, I'll tell you later. Now! Just come."

Julie hung up. "Thank you so much. My sister will be here shortly. Do you have shoes? Looks like I need a pair."

Julie made her sister buy her a pair of very expensive ballet flats. They were teal blue, just the thing for a cruise, Justina assured her. Justina Long had lived in Cold Spring Harbor her entire life. Her parents owned a great deal of the land there, she told Julie. She knew each and every Hemmings that had ever lived in the house, ad nauseam. Julie enjoyed the cup of orange pekoe tea, served in a dainty cup and saucer with Milano cookies, while she waited for her sister.

"But, one of the first, you know, Tessa Hemmings, was the most interesting. She was quite the cat, if you know what I mean. Never married, but had dozens of lovers. Dozens. No man was safe from her," she told Julie with a conspiratorial nod. "She was supposed to marry Gerald Kanning of the Kanning banking family. He died in the war. I guess she waited for him."

Heather pulled up in her Volvo wagon, got out, came inside the shop, and paid the exorbitant amount for the shoes while she stared at Julie's face with worry.

"What happened to you?"

"Oh, Heath, I don't know—"

"Where's Brad?" Heather asked, grasping Julie's elbow firmly to steer her out the shop's door.

"Back at Bedlam. In Bedlam. Yes, he's in Bedlam."

"The house?"

"The nuthouse. I am so sorry I made us buy it. It's haunted. Brad's possessed."

Heather took her arm as they walked toward her station wagon. "OK, Julie, honey, calm down. The house is not haunted. Did you fall? What happened to your face?"

"No, Heather. Stop and look at me. Something is wrong in that house. Something evil. It burned down my home. It tried to kill me."

"Julie, stop! What are you talking about? I'm calling Brad."

Julie grabbed her hand. "You can't; he's one of them."

"OK, Julie. I'm taking you home with me. We'll talk about it when we get there."

Heather set Julie up on the couch with another bracing cup of tea. This one had a spot of eighty-year-old scotch in it. She wrapped her sister in a fluffy quilt and then quietly called Brad from the kitchen to tell him that his wife was in her house.

"She's there!" She heard the relief in Brad's voice. "I'll be right over."

"Slow down. She was hysterical, Brad. What's going on in that house?"

Brad was silent. "Has she told you about her job? She quit her job."

"What? No. I haven't spoken to her since the fire, and she's been so preoccupied with the damn Hemmings place. What the hell is going on?" Heather demanded.

"Whoa, Heather. It's been hectic. She said Mr. Wilson tried to assault her."

"What! That bastard. I'll kill him," Heather said with venom.

"Get in line, Heather. I want to rip out his heart," Brad growled. "Anyway, she quit the job. She's never going back there, so she's out of danger. I'm coming to get her."

"Give me an hour. Let me calm her down."

Brad made a noise. "All right. OK. See you soon."

Heather came into the living room, a tray of sandwiches in her hands. "What's going on, Jules?"

Julie opened her mouth to say something, floundered, and closed it with a snap. Then she began again. "I'd like to tell you, honest. I don't know where to start."

"Start at the beginning." Heather punched an overstuffed pillow and sat back with her tea, her eyes never leaving her sister's face. "Eat a sandwich," she commanded.

"You're going to think I'm crazy."

"That's beside the point. I know you're crazy. Now, what has been going on?"

Julie related the last two weeks, leaving out nothing, not even the strange out-of-body lovemaking.

"Listen, I'd understand sex with a ghost if your husband looked like mine, but Brad's a hunk."

"He wasn't Brad," Julie insisted. "And it wasn't me. It was like I sharing my body with some other person."

"Did Brad experience it as well?"

"Yes. No. I don't know. We didn't talk about it. I mean, it felt too crazy to even entertain, but then his eyes turned red." Julie shivered.

"Maybe it was just the light. Look, he's on the way here."

"What? I'm not going back there. I can't."

"You can't what?" Brad walked into the room, his hair wild, his eyes concerned.

"They don't look red to me." Heather motioned to her sister.

"They were glowing," Julie insisted, but she felt the fear leaving her.

Brad shucked off his jacket to sit next to her, his face worried. "She's been overwhelmed with the house, her job, the expenses."

Heather nodded. "The fire didn't help."

"Don't talk about me like I'm not here," Julie said, but the fight was out of her.

Brad took her hand, kissing the knuckles. "Don't ever do that again. You're scaring me, Jules."

Tears welled in her eyes. "I'm scaring you! I was locked in the room. It was like at the fire. There was a lady trapped in the wall, and when I ran downstairs, you laughed, and your eyes…they—"

"OK, stop. Come home. You'll get a good night's sleep, and things will look different in the morning."

"I am not going back there. Not ever," Julie told him with finality.

CHAPTER NINETEEN

1862

Gerald heard the muffled singing of the escapees under the tarp. He knew they were stifling, and it was dangerous for them to make noise, but they were alone, and he guessed the song brought them some relief from both fear and grief. The roan mare nickered; the sun peeked through the clouds to dapple the trees with color. The air was rich with the smells of spring. He headed up the Jericho Turnpike toward the city and on to Westchester. There was no one out, the road empty, the hour early.

But it wasn't long before he had company. He heard the intruders before he saw them. There were four of them; they were lined up before him, blocking the road. He turned his head back slightly, telling the fugitives to be quiet. Gerald put his gun on the seat next to him. He slowed the wagon, his eyes wary. He recognized the bounty hunters from earlier.

"Can I help you boys?" he inquired politely.

"We can do this real easy, Lieutenant. You can give up your parcels real gentlemanlike, and we'll be on our way."

"Don't know what you're talking about," Gerald replied. "I'm on army business."

"What kind of business?" the man with the mustache asked.

"Whatever it is, it's none of your business."

"Don't reckon so, son."

"I'm not your son. Now move out of the way and leave me alone."

"I don't think so, boy. You got some fugitive slaves on that wagon, and my job is to bring them home."

"You have no sovereignty here. I am taking supplies to Connecticut."

Two of the bounty hunters dismounted and split off, walking slowly to either side of the wagon. The lead man with the mustache flicked back his duster to reveal his sidearm.

"Don't threaten me, sir," Gerald told him, his hand resting on his weapon. "I'm on army business. You'll hang for this."

Their eyes locked. As if in slow motion, Gerald watched the other man's hand move to his gun. Gerald grabbed his own, raising it simultaneously. Three shots were fired; the acrid smell of gunpowder permeated the air. He watched everything tilt and felt his body falling sideways. There was no pain, only a surprising coldness freezing his limbs. From a distance, he saw that his bullet had hit the other man in the arm. He was weaving in the saddle, looking disturbingly large from Gerald's viewpoint.

One of the men bent down to touch Gerald's neck. The other was pulling back the tarp, exposing the frightened fugitives soon to be made slaves again.

"He dead?"

"Deader than a doornail. He never saw it coming. How's your arm?"

"I'll live. You pay his cousin."

"Yep, the man earned it." He spit a stream of tobacco juice onto the dirt, mounted his horse, and grabbed the reins of his partner's. "Told us the route."

"Well, I guess we better head south."

The bounty hunter beside the wagon threw the tarp over the escapees, then climbed onto the seat and snapped the reins. They turned, leaving Gerald on the road, a gaping wound in the side of his head, a look of surprise on his face.

CHAPTER TWENTY

"**I** said I'm not going back there. That house is haunted. There, I've said it. It's a haunted house."

"Julie!" Heather protested. "Stop that. You are so much better than this."

Brad sighed. "Look, I'll call Sal. His girlfriend works for that medium you talked about. If she comes with us to the house, will you come home?"

"It isn't home, Brad. I thought you hated the house."

"I did. I do. Well, it's been kind to us," he said.

"Are you nuts? What are you talking about?"

"The crap we've pulled out of there. We stand to make a considerable amount of money. I feel like the house is sort of saving us. Come home with me, Julie."

Julie looked at his face, the lines of worry around his eyes. She put her hand in his, asking, "You'll call the lady, Georgia?"

Brad pulled out his phone and dialed Sal. "Hi. Yeah, fine. Listen, Sal, you think you can ask Molly if she can get the psychic out to Bedlam House? Just because. For Julie. OK, call me back." He turned to his wife. "He's calling. He said he's sure he can get her out there. She was interested in the house when he had coffee with her last week."

"He had coffee with her?" Heather asked. "Small world."

"What should I do?" Julie asked her sister.

"You know what you should do. You belong with Brad. Go home, Julie. Go confront your ghosts."

"You don't believe me?"

"I think you believe you've had a ghostly encounter. But, honestly, I think you're just overtired."

"Come with us, Heather. Maybe if you're there, you'll see it, too."

"Just go with Brad. Call me." Heather kissed her sister. "It will be fun—the psychic—go on."

Brad's phone rang loudly. It was Sal. Georgia Oaken had agreed to visit them tomorrow morning. Everybody was looking forward to it. Sort of.

CHAPTER TWENTY ONE

Marum paced the landing, her glittery eyes serious. "What if she sees us?"

"She can't," her companion assured her.

"But she's good. I've seen her on television. She communicates with the dead."

He stayed her with his white hand. "She's very talented, Marum, but it doesn't change the fact that we are not dead. It's simply unprecedented. She'll never be able to figure out who we are."

"Sten, I have trouble figuring out who we are."

Sten held out his hand to take hers. "No, you don't, Marum. You are reminded of it each and every day we are here. You know just why we are here." He blinked, and they disappeared into the ether.

Julie was skittish. Brad almost suggested she take one of the pills the doctor had prescribed after she was burned. They stopped on the way home at the tiny Japanese restaurant in town, splurging like they were still dating and not buried under all their bills. She barely ate the sushi, her favorite. She pushed the tuna around on her plate until Brad reached over and popped it into his mouth.

"I can't waste them, Julie. They're too expensive," he told her with an embarrassed shrug.

"That's why I married you, for your Yankee frugalness." Julie pushed her plate away.

"And here I thought it was because of my rugged good looks," Brad joked.

"Nope, all wrong," Julie said softly. "It was the size of that heart of yours."

Julie was so quiet; it was doing some strange thing to that big old heart of Brad's. She remained silent as New England granite, so he gave her enough space to relax. He had wanted to share the news about the lampshade, but decided to keep the information to himself. Until Sal sold some of the items from the house, he didn't want to tell his wife of their purported worth. He didn't want to get her hopes up. Brad had stopped thinking of all the stuff as junk after Sal mentioned the value of the lampshade. Brad was a solid-as-concrete, cash-on-the-barrelhead, put-your-money-where-your-mouth-is kind of guy. Until he was positive of something, he wouldn't commit. Julie was so opposite—flighty, impulsive—and he knew they both shared being headstrong.

They were opposites, but they do say opposites attract. Julie had come from a comfortable home. She had been pampered. Brad was used to being poor. He had been his entire life. He had lived in rural Maine in a house his great-grandparents had built. He still owned it. He came from a family of fishermen, but overfishing and low profits had put his family out of business just after he finished school. He joined up because it was the only way he could get a job. He stayed because he realized he liked the camaraderie of his brothers in the army. After his second tour, the senselessness of war got to him, and he retired. Willy invited him to New York. Other than his parents' home, there was nothing except solitude in Maine for him. Jobs were scarce. He met Julie three weeks later and knew he'd never be alone again. He loved her. She could be annoying, aggressive in a way he'd never seen in a woman, bossy, and demanding, but he knew his heart had found a home with her. Once they had a few bucks, he wanted to bring Julie to Maine and restore the old place for summers. It was also on a coast, but not like Long Island. It was wind-whipped and rugged, isolated from the world, a perfect place to enjoy silence. He loved that house and hoped that Julie would love the quiet peace of it, too.

They held hands as they mounted the steps to the old house. Julie leaned close to him, whispering, "I'm afraid."

"Of what?" he asked, looking at her white face in the moonlight.

Julie shrugged her shoulders, hesitant to tell him, her eyes downcast.

"Tell me." He shook her.

"You're different in there. It's like I don't recognize you."

Brad knew what she was talking about. He opened his mouth to say something, but couldn't quite get the thoughts into words. She was asking him to admit that he believed something was going on. The logical side of Brad warred with Julie's fanciful nature. It didn't matter that he figured there were explanations; Julie thought it was real.

"Look, I'll sit up all night and watch over you."

Julie's rigid stance melted. Brad was her rock. Dependable, reliable, unshakable.

"You worked all day. I can't let you do that."

"This ain't my first rodeo, baby. I pulled many all-nighters in the service. If it makes you feel safe, then I won't close my eyes at all."

Julie hugged him, a sob escaping her lips.

"I promise you, Jules, I'll keep you safe. If you can't feel secure in your own home, then where will you ever?" he told her.

"I thought you hated this place." She looked up into his face with consternation.

He kissed the top of her head. "Anywhere you are is my home. Besides," he said, turning to look at the great hulking shadow of the house, his arm protectively around her, "it's beginning to grow on me."

"You have got to be kidding me!" Julie shouted. "I want to go to my sister's."

"And sleep where, between Heather and her husband?"

She looked up at her husband's face. He seemed the same, but something was different. He rubbed her arms, warming her, making Julie feel safe. They both stared up at the house, each with a new perception.

"It's a nuthouse," Julie said, seeing the house she loved in a new light.

Brad stayed true to his word. He tucked Julie in their air mattress and dimmed the lights. She watched him light a fire in the fireplace, taking comfort in the smell of the burning wood. She watched his strong face, limned by the amber glow of the blaze, his eyes narrowed as he tended the fire. The wood popped, sending sparks to light up the dim room like fireflies.

Brad padded back, his jeans slung low, his shirt unbuttoned. She watched the play of muscle and bone, his shirt taut as it pulled across his shoulder blades while he worked. He threw a bedroll next to her and then reclined on it.

"Go to sleep." He reached over to brush the hair out of her eyes. "I told you I will watch over you," he whispered.

"You don't have to do this." Julie patted the bed next to her. "Come to bed."

"You're not scared anymore?"

"I'm terrified, but it's not fair."

"Don't worry about fairness. I want you to rest. Tomorrow, maybe this person, what's her name—"

"Georgia," Julie supplied.

"Georgia will bring your mind some ease. I promise you, Jules, I will be here all night. You are safe. Safe as houses."

"Safe as houses?"

"Just some stupid homily my mom used to say when I was a kid," he told her with a gentle smile.

Julie's eyes drifted shut. She was exhausted. Brad lay back, watching both his wife and the fire, content and strangely at peace for the first time in the house.

163

Tessa's vaporous form flitted around the room. She dashed from one corner to the other. Gerald watched from above the fireplace. The human didn't notice her. Tessa got braver. She flew in front of him, disturbing the air enough for Brad to wave his hand as though an insect were bothering him.

"You're getting nowhere, Tessa. He doesn't see you," Gerald said softly.

"I had her gone." She faced Gerald, her visage contorted with anger. "I scared the woman off."

"Why, Tessa? Why are you doing this? Didn't last night mean something to you?"

Tessa landed next to Brad, running her ghostly fingers down his spine, her face sublime. "You thought that was enough for me? You expected me to run off with you to some dismal eternal place and be satisfied? I used you both. I may be done with you, but I'm not finished with him!" She laughed, her face twisted, turning an ugly shade of magenta.

Gerald looked at her, seeing Tessa for who she really was. He stood. "I've wasted both my life and whatever this is to wait for you, Tessa. I can't do this anymore. I just can't."

"So leave," she told him. "Nothing is stopping you. The Sentinels won't prevent *you* from leaving." She dismissed him to wrap her arms around Brad. Whispering into his ear, she watched her prey sit up, his eyes keenly aware of his surroundings. He brushed his hair back, effectively pushing off her embrace. Tessa withdrew to a spot over the mantel, a pout marring her once-pretty face. She hadn't realized that Gerald was gone.

The Sentinels watched the scene unfold from above.

"So this is where it ends?" Marum asked incredulously. "After all this time, you're letting Gerald leave without her?"

"It will all come together again tomorrow," Sten told her with confidence. "Just watch." He motioned to Brad. "All roads lead to tomorrow."

Brad sat up, alert to a subtle change in the air. Carefully, he stood, peering through the darkness, and walked slowly to the simmering air. He leaned closer, his brain telling him it was a mirage or a reflection from the fire. The air was dazzling, sparkling with a luminescence as if lightning bugs were dancing in the room, synchronized, with bursts of color. He stopped, shell-shocked, as the light outlined a voluptuous woman, her body eerily familiar. The face took shape—a strong chin, determined and proud, with a long, aristocratic nose.

Tessa smiled seductively, preening when she realized the man was frozen in his tracks. She began to dance, dropping her creamy shoulders enough so that her décolletage slipped, revealing her ample charms. She lifted her draping skirts, showing off her long legs, the garters tied just above her knees. The little black bows teased every male she showed them to. *Hah*, she laughed, *let humans think they can mesmerize men with a stupid dance on a pole*. She was a master at this; she could capture him with one hand tied behind her back. She swayed closer, her ghostly skirts brushing against him. His eyes were wide, glued to the apparition, his mouth open just a bit. Tessa caressed his startled face, putting her mouth lightly over his.

"Just a taste," she told him coquettishly. "Just a tease to show you the delights to come."

Clouds of red-gold hair framed the alabaster face, fanning away as if a breeze wafted before her. She gyrated her hips invitingly, smiling at Brad. She was beautiful, overblown in a Jessica Rabbit kind of way. Brad watched her, mirth bubbling up from the pit of his stomach. He turned to Julie, humor warring with disbelief.

"Oh, honey," he told his sleeping wife. "This is what scared you. She can't hold a candle to you." He bellowed with laughter.

Tessa's smiled faded; she whimpered and then hissed in disbelief. She turned to look for Gerald. She needed a devoted audience. "Gerald," she called. "Gerald, he's mocking me."

She spun to empty air. The human walked closer, curious but clearly unafraid. The worst part was that he was unaffected by her flirtation. She looked for Gerald. Gerald would make her feel needed. He would make this one realize what he was missing with that skinny scarecrow of a wife. Tessa levitated, screaming for Gerald. If she had a heart, it would beat faster, she knew. The man made her nervous. He wasn't afraid of her—what next? Could he have the power to hurt her like the Sentinels? She needed protection, she needed to feel safe, she needed—Gerald, she realized with a start. She wanted Gerald. She touched the region over her heart, feeling a vast loneliness there. An ache as big as a mountain lodged in the cavity of her chest, making Tessa's arms long to hold him. She flew around the room, searching for Gerald's easy company, his companionship. All those years, she never understood. All those years, and she thought sex was love, lust fulfilling. Her eyes opened wide with the wonder and then the pain.

"Gerald!" She poured all her grief into his name. "Gerald, I never knew it was you, all along. Please, please come back."

Silence stretched before her, like the punishment void. A life of watching other people live their lives, while she observed their joys and even heartaches with no one to turn to for company, to share that moment in time.

Fury unlike any she'd never known, the anger of all her hurt and fear, turned Tessa white with misery. She flew around the room, the speed growing, while she howled in horror at her empty future. She turned on Brad, livid that his lack of fear had brought her to this. She used all her energy to punish. There was no one to check her wild impulses. She roared with the voice of a thousand demons. It erupted in the room, the breath of hell from her open mouth. Brad recoiled. Her twisted face was covered with open sores, the gaping maw that was once pouting lips now a mass of rotten teeth. She opened wide in a wordless scream; a swarm of hornets erupted, changing her face into a grinning skull.

A noise escaped from Brad. His only thoughts were to protect his wife. He raced to the corner of the room and grabbed the machete, swiping it through the onslaught of insects. They parted, surging upward, surrounding the woman and encompassing her so that soon her image was obliterated. There was a flash of light, and the room was empty but for Brad and his wife, his breathing harsh in his ears.

Wide-eyed, he searched the room, tentatively touching the fireplace mantel, his fingers finding the hacked body of a wasp. He shook it out of his hand, wiping his sweaty palms against his jeans. Brad backed away to the mattress. Julie had slept through the whole thing. Easing down, he sat straighter, his diligent eyes watching, the machete in his capable hands.

"He thinks he's the one who got rid of the wasps," Marum stated with a laugh.

"He doesn't know what to believe," Sten responded.

"Where is Tessa? Did you lock her up?"

"There is no reason. Gerald has left; she is alone. Tomorrow she will be attacked. Our plans will finally be fulfilled."

"It's been too long." Marum sighed.

"It is the way of this world. You can't rush them, and they have to think it is all free will."

"It just seems silly."

"It's the only way they learn. What do they say here? 'You can lead a horse to water, but you can't make him drink.'"

"I like the other one better." Marum's silver eyes twinkled. "'You can send a kid to college, but you can't make him think.'"

"Hah, I hadn't heard that one. It sounds more appropriate. They just don't think. They are so tiresome." Sten glanced at Tessa's aura spinning furiously on the banister.

CHAPTER TWENTY TWO

Sleepless nights loved her husband. Julie woke to Brad's haggard but oh so handsome face diligently watching over her. His chin rested in the palm of his hand; he smiled back at her.

"I don't think you're crazy anymore," he told her.

"Well, that's a relief." Julie swung her legs over the side of the mattress. She held out her arms to him and he leaned over, rolling her back to kiss her thoroughly. "Rough night?" she asked.

"You don't know half of it."

"You want to share?"

"I'm not even sure I believe it myself. Let's wait for the medium. We'll revisit the whole thing after she does what she's supposed to do."

"Fair enough."

Brad made coffee while Julie showered and dressed. Sunlight streamed through the windows, the colored glass painting rainbows on the walls. Brad handed Julie her mug, and they observed the changing patterns on the parquet floor.

"Is it my imagination, or does the house seem lighter, happier?" Julie asked.

"I was just thinking the same thing. It's quieter. There was this darkness—"

"An oppressiveness," Julie added.

"Yep. It feels…" Brad couldn't find words.

"Gone," Julie finished lamely.

They heard the front door open. Julie looked at Brad, alarmed.

"I unlocked it while you were in the shower. Babe, this is Cold Spring Harbor." He smiled, his unshaven cheek dimpled.

"Hello, Brad." It was Sal, followed by two women. Julie recognized his girlfriend, Molly. She was a full-bodied blonde with masses of wild, overbleached hair. She had bright blue eyes and a sprayed-on tan. A hand with long bloodred fingernails reached out to take hers.

"Julie."

"Hi, Molly." Julie leaned in to kiss her cheek. "Nice to see you again."

Brad stood against the wall, his long legs crossed, his arms folded over his chest, a white coffee mug in his hands. He nodded a greeting.

A short woman with a long flowing dress wandered in. She smiled a greeting, but her eyes darted around the room. Brad noticed that her hair was two-toned. The back of her head had black hair, the front a shock of white. She greeted them both but seemed distracted. They heard the sound of Willy's heavy boots entering.

"Are we having a party?" Willy asked, taking in all the guests.

"You didn't get the memo? You were supposed to bring doughnuts," Brad told him with a laugh.

"Shoot, ain't she that lady from the TV show?"

"Yup. Georgia Oaken, this is my wife, Julie, and our partner, William Watson. I'm Brad Evans." He held out his hand.

Georgia took it, her keen eyes studying him, and then she turned to peruse the others at length.

"What can we do to help?" he asked.

"You don't have to do anything," Molly informed them. "Georgia's got to get a feel for the place. Give her a minute." She edged close to Julie. "She's been dying to get in here. They say this house is a hotspot for spectral activities. Has been for years. That's why they couldn't sell it. Paul Russo, my selling partner, had an exclusive on this listing for years. He finally gave up on it. And he never gives up on anything."

Molly kept talking. Julie shook her head without really listening, eyes on the medium.

Georgia walked from room to room, touching the walls, her head cocked as though she were listening. She took a pad and pencil from Molly and absently drew strange lines or circles.

Willy opened his mouth to speak, but was warned by Molly not to say anything.

Georgia circled the main hallway and closed her eyes, her face puzzled.

"There's a woman. She's very rooted here. A trouble-maker, you know. She wants you." She opened her bright brown eyes to settle on Brad with astonishment. "Not that I can blame her, but what's she going to do with you? I mean, she's dead, right? Oh, she's trouble, all right. She's been dead, like, forever, but she never left."

"How she know all this?" Willy demanded nervously.

"You." She pointed a stubby purple fingernail at Willy. "You channeled something here that nobody else felt, right?"

Willy gulped and shook his head no.

"Oh yes, you did. It scared you, but they were just reliving the end." She turned her head and walked over to one wall of the salon, touching the dark paneling. "Someone was secretly buried here. You wouldn't believe it." She turned to them. "Listen, in a palace in England, there is a corridor, you know? They say that when you walk in this hallway of the palace, you can see and hear one of Henry the Eighth's wives screaming for him."

"Catherine Howard," Julie said softly. "They say she haunts the hall and relives a moment in time over and over again. King Henry refused to see her, and it is said that when she knew he was outside the room, she ran out, calling him. He ignored her and later beheaded her."

"Right, only it's not her ghost. It's a spectral memory."

"What?" Brad asked.

"A thumbprint in time," Georgia said.

This earned him a knowing "I told you so" look from his wife.

"So there are no ghosts here?" Brad looked doubtful, making Julie wonder what had gone on last night.

"I didn't say that. Willy experienced a spectral memory. There is a spirit who relives his death here every so often. Something in Willy triggered it."

"Like an instant replay?" Willy asked.

"Just so." Georgia touched her leg. "He was wounded." Her breath caught in her throat. "Oh my God, he was an escaped slave. He was hiding here."

Molly interrupted, "It's rumored that there was an Underground Railroad station somewhere here in town. I always assumed it was the Friends Meeting House in Jericho."

"It was here," Georgia told her with finality.

"But you said there was a woman," Brad insisted.

"Well, yes." She wandered to the staircase. "Wait, I don't know what these things are. Wait a minute." She paused.

"What?" Sal demanded.

"There's a man. Oh, oh, he's so sad. The female is back." She looked at Sal, a laugh escaping her lips. "You wouldn't believe what she's doing to you."

Molly moved possessively to him, leaning close. Sal looked at her, put his arms around her, and said, "Worried, sweetheart? You don't have to be. You're the only one in the world for me."

Georgia's eyes traveled upward. "She's not happy." Her voice trailed off and she turned.

Sal whispered into Molly's ear, "Why'd she stop talking? What's going on?"

"Shhh." Molly shushed him. "Let her listen."

Georgia watched the two figures meet at the top landing. She tried to discern more, but it was too dark for her to distinguish anything other than a male and a female floating above them all.

Gerald stood stock-still. He wanted to reach out to take Tessa in his arms. Her shoulders were hunched in defeat. She sensed him before seeing him.

"You came back?" Tessa's voice was small.

"Do you want the truth?" he asked.

"You never left," Tessa answered as she reached out to him. "I…I missed you. I never knew that I could… miss you." Her voice trailed off in shame.

"That's not enough anymore, Tessa," Gerald told her firmly. "I am not going to stay here any longer."

Tessa shook her head. "I understand now. All those years wasted. I never understood."

"You never gave me a chance."

"I took you for granted. You were right in front of me, and I never saw you. All those men. I know now I was searching for something, and I never realized it was you."

"I love you, Tessa."

"I know, and what's more, I know now that I love you. I want to be with you, only you, wherever you take me."

Gerald held out his hand. Tessa placed hers on top of his palm.

"The house was never haunted, was it, Gerald?"

"No, my own, you were the only one haunted here. Let's put it all to rest and see where destiny takes us, together."

"Yes," Tessa echoed. "Together."

They lifted their faces to the sun shining through the stained glass window, leaping together, without fear.

Georgia wiped her streaming eyes, coming back to the silent room. They surrounded her quietly, watching, waiting for her to say something.

"It's over," she told them. "They've left."

"What! That's it?" Willy exclaimed. "But you didn't do nothing!"

Georgia smiled at him. "I didn't have to. She moved on. She finally accepted the help she needed and moved on."

Brad walked over from the doorframe. "You saw her?"

"Red-gold hair and all."

Brad's face paled. "What was this all about?"

Georgia shrugged. "I don't have all the answers. There was a troubled spirit. She'd been here for years. She couldn't move on."

"Move on where?" Julie asked.

"Wherever she needed to. Some call it heaven. Who knows? Either way, she found her peace."

"Why was she doing what she did to us? Not that I mind that she's gone," Julie assured her.

"Why does anybody bully or torment someone else? She was searching for something, and I think she finally found it."

"What?" Julie asked, moving into Brad's arms.

"Love. It's the great equalizer. Isn't being loved or cherished enough to bring anyone peace? Sometimes I find that there was no haunted house, but a haunted heart."

Georgia smiled. "I think my work is done, but there is something else. I don't know exactly what I'm feeling."

"Oh, here we go again!" Willy said with exasperation. "Did my spectral ghoul leave?"

"I don't feel anyone else in the house," she said, though her voice did not sound certain. "Yes." She looked up. "I'm satisfied."

"She's talented," Marum observed.

"No more than the sibyl in Greece or that fellow Nostradamus," Sten responded. "I think we can back off for now. This group seems capable of thinking they are running their own lives."

"Tessa?"

"Has gone to Gerald and her reward. She had to see what was right in front of her to move on. Gerald will take care of her from now on."

"What about us?" Marum backed into the dark shadows, her voice distant. "Is this all there is?"

"You knew that when you took this job," Sten told her. "I always told you never to get attached to them. It's just a job, Marum. Just a job."

"Do you ever get tired of it?" Marum asked, her eyes filled with unshed tears.

"Nah, there is always another one struggling for help. A lost sheep that requires a nudge in the right direction. We can lie low for now. They won't be needing us until their second son is born. He is a hell-raiser and they will need guidance. They are on the right course. I was thinking of a little vacation. Olympus, you know." He winked, and they were lost to time once again.

CHAPTER TWENTY THREE

B rad and Julie held hands, watching with bated breath as the Tiffany lampshade was placed gingerly on a granite stand by a gloved Sotheby's agent. The place was packed with buyers. They had netted close to $400,000 just on the contents of the boxes they had found in the tiny walled-off room. In their wildest dreams they had never expected anything like this to happen. It just couldn't get any better, Julie thought, could it?

"Signed by Louis Comfort Tiffany, rare lotus glass lampshade. I will start the bidding at one-point-five million dollars." The auctioneer hit the lectern with his gavel.

Sal turned to a sea of upraised paddles held by people eager to buy. "Wow," he said in awe.

Apparently, Julie giggled, it could!

Epilogue

J ulie rested her hands on the bulk of her belly. Brad was on a ladder adjusting the sign. It was beautiful, forest-green with bright gold lettering. They had fought over the name, but in the end, she agreed that his choice had a certain charm. The Sleep Inn said it all. It didn't matter if they never had a single customer. The house had made them richer than they could have ever imagined.

Willy had married Rita, and LaMarr was in the process of becoming a big brother. Julie and Brad had had their first big gig last week. Molly's boss, Paul Russo, had his daughter's christening done at the house; his second wife and their blended family looked adorable. Sal and Molly were planning a summer wedding using the Inn's gardens. It had gotten National Trust status when they delved deeper into its Underground Railroad past, and the town had put up a plaque.

Well, Julie was happy. She loved unconditionally and was loved unconditionally. And it seems that in the end, that's all that matters, really.

Author's Note

This was a fun book to write. While there is a Bedlam Street in Cold Spring Harbor, there is no Bedlam or Hemmings House. There are many beautiful homes along the Gold Coast that gave me the inspiration for this mansion.

General McClellan really did work for the Illinois Central Railroad before the war. He was general in chief for the Army of the Potomac. Well loved and respected by his troops, he was at odds with both Lincoln and his staff, causing him to be fired. It was said that he was influenced by the information given to him by Pinkerton scouts.

While looking for information about the Underground Railroad, I was amazed to discover that the Maine Maid Inn, right off Jericho Turnpike in Jericho, New York, was indeed a safe house. Valentine Hicks was a known station master and used his home to help slaves escape north. The Maine Maid Inn has recently been given protected status as a historical site by the town of Oyster Bay.

49210673R00111

Made in the USA
Charleston, SC
21 November 2015